A MERCHANT CALLED LYDIA

THE CALLED
BOOK 5

KENNETH A. WINTER

WildernessLessons

JOIN MY READERS' GROUP FOR UPDATES AND FUTURE RELEASES

Please join my Readers' Group so i can send you a free book, as well as updates and information about future releases, etc.

See the back of the book for details on how to sign up.

A Merchant Called Lydia

"The Called" – Book 5 (a series of novellas)

Published by:

Kenneth A. Winter

WildernessLessons, LLC

Richmond, Virginia

United States of America

kenwinter.org

wildernesslessons.com

Edited by Sheryl Martin Hash

Cover design by Scott Campbell Design

ISBN 978-1-9568660-5-6 (soft cover)

ISBN 978-1-9568660-6-3 (e-book)

ISBN 978-1-9568660-7-0 (large print)

Library of Congress Control Number: 2022909537

DEDICATION

In memory of my mother,
Betty Winter,
a woman of grace and beauty,
who lived her life with the courage and strength of Lydia.

She loved her husband, her children, her grandchildren,
and her great-grandchildren well,
and
she desired for everyone she met to know the One she loved the most,
her Lord and Savior, Jesus Christ.

∽

A woman who fears the LORD will be greatly praised.
(Proverbs 31:30)

∽

CONTENTS

From the author   viii
Preface   x

1. A Roman city   1
2. My Macedonian heritage   5
3. My Roman heritage   8
4. Growing up in Thyatira   12
5. My Roman education begins   16
6. A grand welcome in our honor   20
7. Busy days and an unexpected overture   24
8. The years pass quickly   28
9. The day arrives   32
10. The surprise that awaited me   37
11. A life is given, and a life is taken   41
12. Searching for the unknown   45
13. My arrival in Philippi   49
14. Gathering for prayer   53
15. An unexpected visitor at the river   57
16. Come and stay at my home   61
17. Wrongfully punished   65
18. A church is born   69
19. The church grows   73
20. My return to Thyatira   77
21. Resistance from the guilds   81
22. Returning to Rome   85
23. Arrested!   89
24. News from Philippi   93
25. My return to Philippi   97
26. A city in flames   101
27. Finishing my race   105

Please help me by leaving a review!   109
You will want to read all of the books in "The Called" series   110
If you enjoyed this story about Lydia …   111
Through the Eyes   112
The Eyewitnesses collection   113
Lessons Learned In The Wilderness   114
Also available as an audiobook   115
Scripture Bibliography   116
Listing of Characters (alphabetical order)   119
Acknowledgments   122
About the Author   123
Please join my Readers' Group   124

FROM THE AUTHOR

A word of explanation for those of you who are new to my writing.

You will notice that whenever i use the pronoun "I" referring to myself, i have chosen to use a lowercase "i." This only applies to me personally (in the Preface). i do not impose my personal conviction on any of the characters in this book. It is not a typographical error. i know this is contrary to proper English grammar and accepted editorial style guides. i drive editors (and "spell check") crazy by doing this. But years ago, the Lord convicted me – personally – that in all things i must decrease and He must increase.

And as a way of continuing personal reminder, from that day forward, i have chosen to use a lowercase "i" whenever referring to myself. Because of the same conviction, i use a capital letter for any pronoun referring to God throughout the entire book. The style guide for the New Living Translation (NLT) does not share that conviction. However, you will see that i have intentionally made that slight revision and capitalized any pronoun referring to God in my quotations of Scripture from the NLT. If i have violated any style guides as a result, please accept my apology, but i must honor this conviction.

Lastly, regarding this matter – this is a <u>personal</u> conviction – and i share it only so you will understand why i have chosen to deviate from normal editorial practice. i am in no way suggesting or endeavoring to have anyone else subscribe to my conviction. Thanks for your understanding.

PREFACE

~

This fictional novella is the fifth book in the series titled, *The Called*, which is about ordinary people whom God called to use in extraordinary ways. As i've said before, we tend to elevate the people we read about in Scripture and place them on a pedestal far beyond our reach. We then tend to think, "Of course God used them. They had extraordinary strength or extraordinary faith. But God could never use an ordinary person like me."

But nothing could be further from the truth. The reality is that throughout history God has used the ordinary to accomplish the extraordinary – and He has empowered them through His Holy Spirit.

Lydia was one of those people. She first appears in Scripture in Acts 16. Prior to our introduction to her, she had already achieved success in business. And though she was a Gentile, she was already seeking to know the God of the Jews. Through these pages, we'll explore how she could have achieved her success, and the possible circumstances in her life that led her to meet the apostle Paul.

Scripture does tell us that Lydia was from Thyatira, the same city refer-
enced by the apostle John in Revelation 2. We read in Acts that Paul and
Silas were prevented by the Spirit from entering Thyatira and the other
cities of Asia on Paul's second missionary journey. It was that journey that
subsequently led them to meet Lydia in Philippi.

i have often wondered if God didn't need them to stop in Thyatira because
their role was to bring the Gospel to Lydia, and her role was then to bring
the Gospel back to Thyatira. This story explores that possibility.

Also, you will see that the city of Rome plays an important role in this
storyline. There is no indication in Scripture – or anywhere else, for that
matter – that Lydia spent any time in Rome. It is a fictional device i have
employed in the story to help describe how the cities of the empire were
ruled by Rome, and how the city became the scene for significant events in
the early history of the church.

Lastly, the story concludes just prior to the apostle John addressing the
Thyatiran church in the Book of Revelation. It gives us a view of an impor-
tant kingdom principle in the mission of God and the spread of the
Gospel.

So, sit back and enjoy this walk through the life of Lydia and the others
who surround her. Many of the characters in the story come directly from
Scripture. You will recognize many of them from the pages of the Book of
Acts, the Epistles written by Paul, and the Book of Revelation. In
numerous instances, i have added background details about them that are
not in Scripture so we might see them as people and not just names. i draw
heavily on the historical writings of Josephus in doing so. But please
always remember that i employ plausible fiction as well.

As in my other stories, i have added completely fictional characters to
round out the narrative. They often represent people we know existed but
are never given any details about, such as parents or children. Included in

the back of this book is a character map you can use to clarify the historical vs. fictional elements of each character.

Whenever i directly quote Scripture during the story, it is italicized. The Scripture references are also included as an appendix in the book. Those remaining instances of dialogue related to individuals from Scripture, such as Paul, that are not italicized are a part of the fictional story that helps advance the narrative.

One of my greatest joys as a biblical teacher and author is when readers tell me they were prompted to go to the Bible and read the biblical account after reading one of my books; i hope you will do so. None of my books is intended to be a substitute for God's Word – rather, i hope they will lead you to spend time in His Word.

Finally, my prayer is, that as you read this story, you will see Lydia through fresh eyes – and be challenged to live out *your* walk with the Lord with the same boldness, humility, and courage she displayed. And most importantly, i pray you will be challenged to be an "ordinary" follower with the willingness and faith to be used by God in extraordinary ways . . . for His glory!

∾

1

A ROMAN CITY

∾

"Lydia, Macedonian blood flows through your veins. Be true to your heritage, and honor your Macedonian forefathers." My father began telling me that when I was just a toddler, though I didn't understand what he meant. Our city – the city of Thyatira – had very much become a Roman city.

Thyatira is surrounded by hills and lies in the mouth of a long valley that flows north from the Hermus River. We are fortunate that our fertile land remains fruitful without the hard work required in more parched regions of Asia. A continuous procession of camels transports Thyatira's produce to the bazaars of Pergamos, Sardis, and Smyrna.

Prior to its colonization by Macedonian King Seleucus Nicator, Thyatira was a small farming village, sparsely populated and clustered around a central pagan temple. But the Macedonians viewed Thyatira as a strategic military outpost. They believed it was key to protecting the great trade highway that wound through the valley.

Because of Thyatira's key location, they believed the protection of their rule and their provincial capital of Pergamos rested on the strength of our city. As a result, the fortunes of Pergamos and Thyatira were inextricably linked from that day forward.

The Macedonian soldiers brought little in the way of possessions with them, but they did bring their worship of the sun god Apollo to our city. The temple constructed in his honor is one of the few Macedonian structures that remain in the city today.

Though Thyatira was viewed as a gateway into Asia, it was never a fortified city. No one would ever mistake it as a powerful ruling city. Instead, our purpose was to protect whichever empire we happened to belong to at the time by preventing the enemy from penetrating deeper into imperial territory.

That all changed, however, when we became a part of the Roman Empire. Emperor Augustus instituted changes that enabled our city to blossom and prosper into the thriving city we are today. The Roman Empire, with its vast military might, did not view our location as a strategic military outpost; instead, they regarded us as a valuable city of industry and trade. Our city soon teemed with foundries for the production of brass and bronze instruments. Sweltering artisans toiled over white-hot flames fashioning Thyatiran wares that were coveted throughout the empire.

But those were not the only significant items produced in our city. We also became well-known for our linen and woolen cloth industry – especially our red and purple cloth. Purple is the more costly of the two and is used primarily by those who are wealthy or royal. Red cloth, on the other hand, is more widely used by the masses.

Purple cloth, generally sold throughout the empire, is produced using a dye derived from tiny Mediterranean mollusks found along the Phoenician and Spartan coasts. But the dye produced in Thyatira is refined from the roots of plants uniquely indigenous to our area. The combination of those roots and the waters of our region produce a dye that is a much richer hue and is resistant to fading – making it a more sought-after product.

The current Roman emperor, Vespasian, has done even more to foster the city's growth and prestige, including the addition of three new gymnasiums, an impressive colonnaded stoa of merchant shops and craftsmen stalls, and many more shrines to the Roman gods. We most definitely have come to reflect the best – and the worst – of Rome.

As the city grew in importance in industry, Thyatira became host to numerous guilds centered around the various trades. In fact, there are more trade guilds in our city than in any other city in Asia. The guilds are not solely the center of business life within the trades. If you belong to a guild, your life pretty much functions within the confines of the social, civic, and religious views of the guild, as well.

The three most powerful guilds in our city are the coppersmiths, the bronzesmiths, and the dyers. Those three greatly influence the thinking of our other guilds, which include the wool workers, the linen workers, the makers of outer garments, the leather workers, the tanners, the potters, the bakers, and the slave dealers. As you might expect, a person's position in the community is determined by which guild he belongs to and where he stands in the hierarchy of his respective guild.

Over the years, there has been a blending of races in our city. Our long-standing families are primarily of Macedonian descent. A considerable influx of families of pure Roman descent began to immigrate to the city once Rome took possession of our lands, as did peoples from other regions of the expanding empire. My family is a mixture of the two.

In more recent years, there has been an influx of people from Egypt, Judea, the Arabian Peninsula, Syria, and Cilicia. They have brought their diversity of religious beliefs, including the one perceived by most to be the most unique of them all – the Jews. Over time those beliefs have become syncretized into an amalgamation of beliefs. It has become acceptable to believe whatever you think is true – as long as you do not express the idea that one belief is more correct than another. Emperor Vespasian has even introduced the idea of the deification of Caesar himself.

As such, we have become a tolerant city as long as a person's beliefs do not violate the code of his guild. Yes, we are a city of contradictions, but many would also tell you that we have become a shining city within the empire – wealthy in riches and progressive in our beliefs. It is the city I became proud to call home.

2

MY MACEDONIAN HERITAGE

~

*F*or a brief time under the rule of Alexander the Great, the Macedonian Empire was the most powerful in the world. It was the epicenter from which Greek arts and literature flourished, and the enlightenment of philosophy, engineering, and science spread to the rest of the known world. The great philosopher and teacher, Aristotle, spent most of his adult life in Macedonia in the city of Pella after King Philip brought him there to tutor his son, Alexander the Great.

As my father often reminded me, our Macedonian ancestors were from Pella. He was confident that they too had acquired much of their knowledge from sitting at the feet of Aristotle. Perhaps the great philosopher had gained some of his knowledge from them as well!

After the death of Alexander the Great, the city soon lost its prestige and began to fade into the shadows as a small provincial town. My ancestors, like many others, began looking for opportunities in the new Asian colonies. As a result, when the Macedonian soldiers arrived in Thyatira, they were accompanied by a host of tradesmen and merchants seeking greater fortune. One of my ancestors was counted among their number.

By the time the Romans took control of our city and the surrounding region, four generations of my family had made their mark and prospered in their adopted city. They quickly learned that wealthy families – regardless of which empire they belonged to – always desired to clothe themselves and furnish their homes in the finest fabrics. My family's prosperity came through the discovery of our now infamous Tyrian purple dye.

The Romans had worked tirelessly to extend their empire and develop an expanded infrastructure of trade routes that fostered more opportunities for business. By the time my grandfather was in control of our family business, ours was one of the most prestigious in the city, and he had become one of its most powerful men.

As a matter of fact, my grandfather was instrumental in the establishment of the trade guilds for which Thyatira is famous. And he carefully mentored his son, Evander, preparing him to eventually take over the family business as well as maintain the family's influence in the city. He also wisely determined that our family's influence needed to extend beyond the boundaries of Thyatira into the ever-increasing regions that now made up the Roman Empire.

For that to happen, my grandfather sent his son to Rome – the seat of power for the empire – to further his education. But father and son both knew it would also afford him the opportunity to build solid relationships with powerful Roman families, which would be very beneficial in the days ahead. So, at the age of twelve, my father set sail on a merchant vessel bound for Rome.

The voyage was to take a little more than three weeks. It was quite a venture for a twelve-year-old boy to make without his family, but my father was not just any boy. By that age, he had already demonstrated a wisdom beyond his years and a capability to inspire and lead others – even those much older – to accomplish more than they had ever envisioned.

That ability was soon put to the test on his journey. Halfway through the voyage, about three days from their next port of call, Rhegium, a typhoon struck. The captain and crew bravely battled the storm; they enlisted the help of the eight passengers onboard, including my father, to throw the ship's cargo overboard and band the ship's hull.

On the third day of battling the destructive winds and waves, the captain was struck on the head by a damaged mast and swept overboard. He immediately disappeared in the violent waves; there was no time to rescue him.

Without the captain to give them direction, the crew began to panic as the day wore on. They believed the ship was doomed as it tossed to and fro in the waves. When they finally spotted land, they were afraid the ship would not make it through the shoals.

They quickly assessed their situation. The crew feared for their lives if they remained on the ship. They also knew they would not be paid since the captain and cargo were both lost at sea. There was one lifeboat aboard with room enough for the crew but no passengers. So, they decided to give the passengers a task to distract them while several crew members lowered the lifeboat to make their escape.

My father, however, noticed what the crew was doing and alerted the other passengers. He knew that without the crew the ship would be lost. Without any hesitation, he made his way to the stern, picked up a knife along the way, and cut the rope securing the lifeboat to the ship. When the crew realized what he had done and saw there was no way to reach the lifeboat, they ran toward him to throw him overboard.

3

MY ROMAN HERITAGE

~

*B*ut in the heat of the moment, my father called out, "I believe the only chance we have in surviving this storm is if we all stay together. You men have the experience and know-how to guide this ship to land, and the eight of us will add our strength to the effort. We passengers know that with the loss of the captain and cargo you will not be paid for this voyage. But we will all pay you a reward equal to three times what you would have received if you guide us to dry land!

"You know that your chances in that small lifeboat were not much better than on this ship. But if we all work together, we might just be able to tell the story to our children of how we survived this storm! And you men will be paid handsomely for the effort!"

As my father spoke, the crew members looked at one another. The men who had grabbed him relaxed their grip. Slowly, they all nodded their agreement and turned to look at their first mate.

The first mate asked, "How do we know the rest of these passengers will pay up the money needed to provide this bounty you have promised us?"

All the other passengers looked at him and nodded their heads in agreement. But then my father added, "Because if they don't, I will! You will receive your funds when we get to Rome – and if not, you can hold me captive until you do!"

"Well, young sir," the first mate exclaimed, "we accept your pledge and will hold you responsible to fulfill it. Otherwise, you will pay dearly for having cut that rope!"

Under the direction of the first mate and crew, the ship lurched in to shore the next day. We came aground about an hour's walk southeast of Rhegium, the most southern city on the coast of Italy. As the passengers made their way to the city, they discussed the bounty they had promised to pay the crew. Several men said they should report the crew to the authorities in Rhegium and have them arrested for extortion and abandonment at sea. But my father reminded them they had all given their pledge.

The crew set about locating a ship's captain who needed a crew for a voyage to Rome that also could accommodate eight passengers. It seemed like an impossible request, but unbeknownst to everyone involved, God was ordering their steps and just such an opportunity became available. My father and the other passengers had to pay an additional fare to their new captain to take them to Rome – but at that point, it was a small price to pay to get to their destination.

After docking in Rome, my father accessed the funds his father had already sent ahead to provide for his living expenses. Between those funds and those of the other passengers, they were able to settle their obligation to the sailors before they all parted ways. My father had to live frugally for his first three months. It took that long for word to reach my grandfather of his need for additional funds and for those funds to arrive in Rome.

But his depleted finances did not prevent my father from making inroads into Roman society from his very first day. His wit and charm quickly opened doors with his fellow students as well as their prestigious families. One of those students was a young man named Aurelius, who was the same age as my father. My father was always one step ahead of him – both in the classroom and on the athletic field. But the two students soon became inseparable, and my father became a frequent guest in his friend's home.

Aurelius was the son of Gaius, an influential member of the Roman senate and, as it turned out, a close friend of Emperor Augustus. Each visit to Aurelius's home gave my father the opportunity to meet another member of Rome's elite and solidify his place in that social circle.

But the one who truly captured my father's attention was Aurelius's younger sister, Caecilia. As the years passed, she transformed into the lovely young woman who captured my father's heart. However, unlike her brother, she was never one step behind my father in anything. As a matter of fact, my father often said he knew from the start he would always have to run just to keep up with her!

When Caecilia's father became aware that a relationship was blossoming between his daughter and my father, he made it clear he would not grant his permission for her to marry until she was twenty years of age. He told my father he would not allow her education to be interrupted.

By that time, my father had become firmly established as a member of Roman society and was a leading merchant in the city. Our family's Tyrian purple was now the only acceptable purple dye to be used in the clothing and household linens of the Roman elite, and it was only available through my father. So, neither my grandfather nor my father was in any rush for him to return home to Thyatira. The decision to send my father to Rome had become even more profitable than either of them had imagined.

When he and Caecilia were married, I am told it was one of the major events of that year's social calendar. Everyone who was anyone was in attendance. Even Emperor Augustus and the Empress Livia graced the event with their presence. But my father always told me that event paled in the eyes of both he and my mother in comparison to the occasion that took place just three years later. That was the day my mother gave birth to me.

4

GROWING UP IN THYATIRA

~

*D*uring my father's early years in Rome, he was introduced to a man named Linus, a successful Roman trader in fabrics. He specialized in exotic silks from the Far East and fine linens from the Middle East. He and my father soon realized that between Linus's fabrics and my father's exclusive dye, they could easily control the textile market to the upper class of Rome. Their relationship began as a business partnership but soon the bond between them became even closer than brothers. I even referred to him as my Uncle Linus.

He was the first one to receive the message from Thyatira that my grandfather had died. The merchant sailors who arrived with a shipment of dye also carried the message to my father. Though I was too young to fully understand, I knew my father was heartbroken when Uncle Linus delivered the news.

My father knew that he must return to Thyatira without delay. He needed to comfort my grandmother and take over the affairs of the family business. His sorrow over his father's death was compounded by the sadness both of my parents felt. My mother had never been separated from her family or her beloved Rome, and, after seventeen years, the city had become my father's adopted home. Though my father would always tell me that Macedonian blood flowed through our veins, he also knew that Rome would always hold a special place in his heart.

My parents quickly set about making arrangements for their departure. Uncle Linus would assume full responsibility for their joint business affairs in Rome. Passage was booked on a merchant ship scheduled to leave in three days. My Roman grandparents accompanied us to the ship and bade us a sad farewell. My mother often said they were sadder to see me go than they were to see her leave. At the time, I was their only grandchild!

Our three-week journey was uneventful, and my family soon settled into our new home with my grandmother Marijana. My father took over the family's business affairs without delay, while my mother was left to navigate the transition from the sophistication of Rome to the quaintness of Thyatira. Gratefully, she and my grandmother got along right from the beginning.

Even though I am a Roman citizen by birth, I have no memories of the city from when I was a baby. My earliest memories all begin in Thyatira. Even as a young child, I knew our family was one of the most important families in the city. From the day we arrived, my father was considered a city leader, and my mother set the social standard for what a proper household should be like. Our home was always filled with friends, neighbors, and guests seeking the opinion or the affirmation of my parents. Everyone wanted to be considered their friend, and my parents were gracious and hospitable to each one without regard to station in life.

When I was four years old, my brother Janus was born. Though I never questioned my father's love for me, I knew he was thankful to have a son he could raise to walk in his footsteps. But as the years passed, I was the one who began showing the greater interest in learning the family business.

Both my parents placed great value on education, and our mother taught Janus and me during our early years. I admired her for her understanding and proficiency in the studies of philosophy, mathematics, and history. She taught us to read and write in both Latin and Greek, and she passed on to us her great love for poetry.

When I reached the age of twelve, my father paid to have tutors further my education in the subjects of physical science, mechanics, and economics. But some of my greatest education in those areas came from my father. I would often listen as he carried on conversations about business, politics, and philosophy.

Although our family was not very religious, my father taught us that Greek and Roman gods were contrived to be answers to questions people were unwilling or unable to discover for themselves. He admonished Janus and me that we were above all of that. We had the ability to find our own answers and solve our own problems – we didn't need an imaginary god to do that for us.

As I entered my teens, I began to increasingly favor my mother in appearance. I was taller than most young women my age and had a slender frame. My father frequently told me I was becoming quite beautiful – just like my mother. Janus, on the other hand, closely resembled our father. He was very athletic and ruggedly handsome. But, in other ways, I was the one who truly favored our father. I had his skill in business. I was learning how to deal with people astutely but fairly. And I was learning how to lead others confidently – without being overbearing.

Eventually my father succumbed to my pleas to help him with the family business. He was reluctant at first, but ultimately he recognized my passion and skill for the work. My brother, on the other hand, was content to allow me to take a leading role. He was a hard worker, but he had no interest in being the leader.

"You are just like your mother," my father said to me one day. "I have always known she is smarter than I am. But she has always allowed me to think I am the one who is in charge. However, I know better.

"We need to find a husband for you who will not be intimidated by you. And one who will recognize not only your physical beauty but also the beauty of your mind, your will, and your spirit.

"Your mother and I believe it is time for you to return to Rome to further your education and spend some time with your grandparents there. It has been almost fifteen years since we arrived here in Thyatira. Your mother deserves the opportunity to go back and spend time with her family. The two of you will be setting sail for Rome next week!"

5

MY ROMAN EDUCATION BEGINS

~

*J*anus remained home with my father. Though I relished the opportunity of returning to Rome with my mother, a part of me wanted to stay in Thyatira. I knew my father was hoping Janus, in my absence, would begin to show interest in the affairs of our family business and aspire to lead it one day.

As my mother, two of our servants, and I made the journey across the seas, I couldn't help but wonder if my father secretly hoped I would become so enthralled with Rome – and perhaps even find a husband – that I would lose interest in our family business. Though he knew I had the ability to lead it, he favored leaving control of his business to his son rather than his daughter. I was resolved to win him over to my way of thinking, and I was busily making plans to do so.

Our ship docked at the harbor of Ostia, located on the mouth of the Tiber River, eleven miles downriver from Rome. Mother had sent word of our pending arrival to my grandparents, so they sent servants to meet us and accompany us on the riverboat journey to Rome. They greeted us as soon as we stepped off the ship. They fawned over my mother and reminded me I was only a baby when they had last seen me.

When the city came into view, I forgot everything else on my mind. It was magnificent! I had never seen anything so grand. I now know that the lustre of the city is paid for by the taxes of the working people throughout the rest of the empire. Citizens of Rome pay no taxes; the rest of the empire pays it for them. But that fact was nowhere in my mind as I took in the splendor of all that was before me.

Our family lives in one of the grandest homes in Thyatira, but as we approached my grandparents' palatial home, I suddenly felt very provincial. That was even before we walked inside and I witnessed the lavishly appointed mosaic floors and frescoes. But nothing took my breath away more than the sight of my grandmother, Cornelia. She looked like a queen – but her welcoming embrace of my mother and me immediately caused any apprehension to disappear. My surroundings suddenly felt familiar, and I felt at home!

My grandfather, Gaius, returned home from the senate later that afternoon. Although I was momentarily intimidated by the fact he was one of the most important men in the empire, his broad smile and outstretched arms immediately extinguished my fears.

My grandmother soon began making preparations for a grand celebration to announce my mother's and my return. She told me it would be a premier social event of the season. In the meantime, my mother wasted no time in arranging for three of her best tutors to begin my instruction.

Within the first week, I begged my grandfather to allow me to accompany him to the senate. I wanted to witness where and how our most powerful leaders conducted the business of ruling the empire. I hoped I might get a glimpse of the emperor himself. But my grandfather told me Emperor Tiberius had become a recluse and no longer resided in the city. He had delegated the administration of the empire to his Praetorian prefect,

Sejanus. I could tell from my grandfather's description he did not think very highly of the man.

"The emperor and the senate are supposed to be two co-equal branches of government," my grandfather explained. "But in practice, the actual authority of the senate has become negligible as the emperor holds the true power. Since the rule of Augustus, our authority has slowly been diminished. As such, our position as senators is mainly one of prestige and social standing rather than actual authority. In recent days, Sejanus has orchestrated it so our independent legislative, judicial, and electoral authority is now completely nonexistent. We function solely as a vehicle through which the emperor exercises his autocratic powers."

As the session unfolded, my grandfather pointed out Sejanus as he was addressing the senate. But based upon the speech he was giving, I had already surmised who he was.

Late in the day, as we were leaving the senate chamber, a voice called out from behind us. "Gaius," he bellowed, "who is this young lady with you today?"

We stopped and turned toward the man as my grandfather answered. "Prefect Sejanus, please allow me to introduce my granddaughter, Lydia."

Sejanus bowed, taking my hand in his, and said, "Lydia, it is an honor to make your acquaintance. I had no idea Gaius had a granddaughter . . . and particularly one so beautiful."

"You are most kind, sir," I replied. "My mother and I have only recently arrived in Rome for a visit with my grandparents."

"Ah, yes, you are Caecilia's daughter," he replied with a smile. "I had heard she had returned for a visit, but my sources failed to tell me about you. I hope you will enjoy your stay. I find that most people who come to Rome love it so much they never leave. I hope that will be true of you, as well. Please call on me if I can be of service in any way."

With that, he walked away – after he and my grandfather clearly exchanged contemptuous glares at one another.

6

A GRAND WELCOME IN OUR HONOR

~

"*B*e wary of that man, Lydia," my grandfather warned. "Sejanus is the most powerful man in Rome, second only to the emperor. But he is a treacherous man who is not to be trusted. No matter how much he may ooze charm, his venom is poisonous, and his bite is deadly. Avoid him at all costs."

Since I didn't plan to return to the senate, I thought avoiding him would be no problem.

The next night was the welcome celebration my grandmother had planned for us. It was the second time since my arrival in Rome I felt very unsophisticated. I had never seen such a variety or quantity of exotic foods: pheasant, thrush, oysters, lobster, venison, wild boar, and peacock. In addition, I was told the cooks had prepared two special dishes in my honor: roasted pig stuffed with sausages and hare decorated with wings to resemble Pegasus.

I had also never seen such a large assembly of guests dressed in such finery. To her credit, mother remembered most of their names and greeted each one with her usual grace and charm before introducing me. I worked diligently to follow her lead and remember each name. I realized I was now seeing what her life had been like before she followed my father to Thyatira. It was a very different world!

As the evening progressed, she reintroduced me to Uncle Linus, whom I barely remembered since I was so young when we left Rome. I felt at ease in his company the moment I saw him. He instantly felt like family, and I could see how he and my father had become such good friends and partners.

"Uncle Linus," I asked, "may I come visit you at your place of business? I would like to see all that you are doing here. My father talks of you so fondly and so often."

"It would be my pleasure, my dear," he answered, after first giving my mother a questioning look to make sure it was all right with her. "Let me know what day works best for you, and I will arrange it."

"How about tomorrow?" I replied without hesitating.

My earnestness prompted a chuckle from him before he replied, "You are most definitely your father's daughter! Yes, by all means! Tomorrow it is!"

I was immediately excited about the appointment. My father always told me he credited much of his skill in business to the time he and Uncle Linus worked side by side. I knew I still had much to learn, and I knew my visit would be the beginning of that education. I soon found myself daydreaming about visiting the business as the guests and their chatter faded into the background.

However, I was startled back to reality when I heard someone call my name. "So Lydia, are you enjoying being the center of attention this evening?"

I turned to find myself face to face with Sejanus – and my grandfather was nowhere in sight to come to my rescue. "Prefect Sejanus, I didn't realize I would have the pleasure of seeing you again so soon! It is kind of you to take time out of your busy schedule to join us tonight. You honor my mother and me with your presence."

Suddenly, out of the corner of my eye, I saw my mother approaching. "Have you had the opportunity to meet my mother?" I asked, as I turned to introduce them.

"Yes, your mother and I knew one another before your father stole her heart," Sejanus said, with a sigh of regret. "Caecilia, it is a pleasure to see you again. I know your parents have missed you. I hope you are enjoying your days back here in the city."

"It is a delight to be back and to introduce Lydia to its charms and see the many changes that have occurred in my absence. Not the least of which is how you have risen to a position of such incredible responsibility and authority. I'm sure you must be very proud of your achievements."

My mother continued to flatter him for a few more minutes before she turned to me and said, "Lydia, please go join your grandmother and attend to our other guests while I continue to entertain the prefect. Though he is our most honored guest, we do not want to overlook the others."

Given how awkward I had felt both times around Sejanus, I was grateful to my mother for freeing me from his intimidating gaze. I hastily found my grandmother and shook off the sense of foreboding I felt around the prefect. But as I looked back at them, I noticed their conversation had become a bit animated. Mother looked stern and resolute, and Sejanus looked most displeased.

As I stood watching them, I wondered what they could possibly be discussing in hushed tones. Just then, Uncle Linus and a younger man approached me and captured my attention. "Lydia," Linus began, "my son, Lucius, has just arrived and I would like to introduce him to you."

I could tell Lucius was a few years older than I was, but he and I were most definitely the youngest people in the room. I was pleased to have someone closer in age with whom I could engage in conversation.

He told me he had actually seen me years ago when I was a baby. He was a boy of six when I was born, so his recollection of me was that I was tiny and slept a lot. "Obviously, you've changed quite a lot!" he said somewhat awkwardly.

As the night continued, I learned about his involvement in his father's business and his desire to take it over one day. Our conversation gradually became easier, and I knew we would become good friends.

7

BUSY DAYS AND AN UNEXPECTED OVERTURE

❧

𝒯he next morning, I asked my mother what she and the prefect had been discussing. "Oh, that," she replied. "It was nothing really. Just a misunderstanding related to something that happened years ago. But I'm certain it is settled now, and we will hear nothing more about it!"

Then she deftly changed the subject. "I noticed that you and Lucius seemed to be enjoying getting to know one another. He has grown into such a handsome young man, and his father tells me he is very gifted in business. He reminds me of your father at that age," she concluded with a smile.

As the days and weeks passed, I found myself thinking less about Thyatira and becoming more preoccupied with Rome. I will confess that Lucius probably had something to do with that!

My days began to follow a consistent schedule. In the mornings I would attend to my studies with my tutors. They pushed me to open my mind as

I studied the works of Aristotle. Though he lived almost 400 years before me, his writings on metaphysical philosophy captured my interest as did his theses on psychology and meteorology. And somewhat to my grandfather's chagrin, the tutors, at my mother's direction, pressed me to become even more skilled in debate and oratory.

"All the women in my family are already skilled at debating me on any subject they choose," he sighed. "You don't need any further training in that regard," he added, with a twinkle in his eye and a smile on his lips.

During the afternoons, I was most often with Uncle Linus as he negotiated with his suppliers or charmed his customers. After a time, he began allowing me to take part in the conversations, and we both realized I had a talent for it. I would disarm our suppliers with my youth and gender before I craftily led them to agree to terms that were far better than what my uncle had proposed. More than once they told my uncle that I drove a harder bargain than he did – and he knew they were right.

There was no denying I had the advantage when we were presenting our newest fine linens to our female clientele. They soon accepted that I was an authority on whatever was the most fashionable and durable. Uncle Linus confided to my mother that he was learning just as much from me as I was learning from him. Lucius often accompanied us on those visits, but he soon began to sit back and smile at me as I took control of the conversations.

However, he did take the lead on our evening schedule when he and I attended the galleries and theaters. He had a far greater appreciation for, and knowledge of, the arts than I would ever have. I marveled at his ability to see things in the arts that were much more obscure to me.

One day I asked my grandfather if I could again go with him to the senate, and he agreed to take me. "Grandfather, do you think we will encounter the prefect while we are there?" It was the first I had thought of him since the night of the celebration.

"We will likely see him from a distance," grandfather replied, "but I do not expect he will seek you out."

"I saw that he and mother were having a stern conversation the night he came to our home. Do you know what it was about?" I asked. "Mother would not tell me."

Grandfather hesitated before answering. "Yes, you have a right to know. Years ago, long before Sejanus was prefect and long before your mother and father were married, Sejanus sought my permission to court your mother. I have never trusted the man, even when he was young. But I also knew he would one day rise to a powerful position, so I did not want to offend him. I told him she had her eye on your father, and I had already given my permission to your father to court her, even though I had not yet officially given my blessing.

"He tried unsuccessfully to convince me to change my mind, but at the end of the day, he grudgingly accepted my answer. He and I have been at odds ever since.

"That night at the celebration, since your father is not here, he asked your mother for her permission to court you. There is no question he is the second most powerful man in the empire – at least for now. You would want for nothing, and you would immediately rise to the pinnacle of Roman society. But your mother also knows the man's heart. He is old enough to be your father, but he has absolutely none of your father's good character. Your mother would never agree to allow you to enter into what she knows would become a loveless relationship.

"But your mother also wisely knew to respond carefully. He is the prefect, after all. Many are the men who have been imprisoned – or worse – for having said 'no' to him. She first told him how flattered the family would be to learn the prefect had expressed interest in her daughter. She told him it was a great honor, beyond all imagination! But then she told him you are much too young to enter into such a commitment right now; and regardless, your age difference would prevent your father from ever agreeing to such a union. She again thanked him for honoring you and the family in such a way but told him her answer was 'no.' There could be no further discussion.

"I would venture to say the only person in Rome today who could get away with speaking to him like that is your mother. I believe he still has feelings for her. I believe his interest in courting you was because you are so much like her – in every way. But he uncharacteristically accepted her decision. He would never want the matter to be known publicly because it would damage his reputation if others knew he had been refused. So, he has not mentioned it again. He will now avoid talking to you or acknowledging you in any way. His pride will prevent him from doing so. He needs to treat you with indifference."

"I had no idea!" I told my grandfather. "I owe my mother a greater debt than I could ever imagine – in more ways than one."

8

THE YEARS PASS QUICKLY

~

*T*he first anniversary of our arrival in Rome came around quickly. The year had been a whirlwind of new experiences. Rome had become my home even though I longed to see my father and brother. My heart had been captured by its sophistication, its opportunities, and its openness to new ideas. I found myself with greater prospects than I had ever envisioned in Thyatira. Here I could be the woman I wanted to be – enlightened, cosmopolitan, and successful. Given my youthful outlook, I firmly believed there was no limit to what I could do.

My grandfather was my greatest champion. He encouraged me to stretch my wings and fly. Whenever my grandmother commented I was "stretching" beyond the bounds of propriety for a young woman my age, he would always retort, "The gods have given her wings to stretch those boundaries. She will set the standards by which others will one day aspire to achieve!"

I counted my time with all my family as precious, but I treasured my time with my grandfather the most; we had become very close. That's why the news I received from my mother one afternoon hit me hard. I was working alongside Uncle Linus when I received her message. It read: "Please come home at once. Something has happened!"

My mother was never overly dramatic, so I knew the matter must be urgent and I hurried home. As I entered the house, I saw my mother and grandmother consoling one another. Through her tears, my mother haltingly told me, "Your grandfather collapsed on the senate floor this afternoon. His heart appears to have just stopped. There was nothing anyone could do. Your grandfather is dead."

My legs buckled beneath me. I would have collapsed to the floor if my Uncle Aurelius had not reached out to steady me. He, his wife, Diana, and my younger cousin, Pudens, had also just learned the news and had immediately come to the house. To say we were all in shock would be an understatement. My grandfather had been the picture of health.

The days immediately following were a blur. Because of my grandfather's position in the senate, his funeral took on the magnitude of a public event over multiple days. He was laid out in his finest toga and wore a wreath that reflected his station. Even through my tears, I admired just how handsome he was. His body was placed on display in the main hall of our home for two days before being taken to the senate meeting chamber so the public could pay their respects.

My Uncle Aurelius was given the honor of bringing the public eulogy. I secretly wished I could have done it, but there was no doubt that would have not only been inappropriate but scandalous. My grandfather's cronies told my uncle the eulogy would be a good way for him to show the people he was ready to take his father's place in the senate.

All of Rome's ruling elite were in attendance. Even the prefect made a brief appearance. I watched as he spoke a few quiet words to my mother and grandmother. Though I knew he and my grandfather had never seen eye to eye, I was grateful he had come to pay his respects. I did notice, however, he never even glanced in my direction.

Following the eulogy, a public feast was held to honor my grandfather's memory. It continued for several hours until it was time for the procession to carry his body to the crematory pyre. The streets were lined with people paying their respects. Once his body was cremated, my grandfather's ashes were placed in an urn and interred in the cemetery reserved for the city's elite. My uncle and grandmother commissioned the creation of a suitable monument to mark my grandfather's final resting place.

Our lives gradually settled into a new normal. My father sent his heartfelt sympathies and condolences and asked my mother if he should come join us in Rome. She told him that wasn't necessary, but she would be delaying her return to Thyatira so she could stay and comfort her mother during her time of grief.

My uncle assumed my grandfather's seat in the senate. He and my aunt soon moved into my grandparents' home, taking occupancy as its new master and mistress. We had been in Rome for almost three years when my mother approached me about returning to Thyatira. Though my heart longed to see my father and brother, it longed even more to remain in Rome.

I knew my staying would help soften the absence of my mother for my grandmother. And truth be told, I didn't want to leave Lucius. Though we had not discussed marriage, it was becoming obvious to us, and all those around us, that day was approaching. I had decided I would not marry until I was twenty-one, and that was still two years away. In the meantime, I wanted to continue my education – both in my studies and in business. My mother agreed I should remain.

Lucius and I accompanied my mother to meet the ship that would carry her back to Thyatira. One of my grandmother's servants would be her companion on the voyage home.

Just before my mother boarded the ship, she turned to me and said, "Lydia, when we arrived in Rome, you were a wide-eyed girl. You have become an accomplished young woman with the poise and ability to accomplish anything you set your mind to do. Though I go with a sad heart knowing I am leaving you behind, I go with a heart that could not be prouder of who you are. I know you do not seek a husband *within* whom you will find purpose, but rather one *with* whom you will find purpose together. If you decide Lucius is that one, you have your father's and my blessing.

"Allow Rome to continue to teach you, but do not forget that Thyatira is in your heart. One day you will return to us. And you will know when that day has arrived."

9

THE DAY ARRIVES

~

A year later, when I was twenty, Lucius and I formally announced our engagement. We made plans to marry on my twenty-first birthday. Our engagement seemed to spark new life in my grandmother. She immediately began making all the plans. I was grateful for her help, and she was pleased to have the occasion to occupy her mind. Though I was no longer the unrefined sixteen-year-old who had arrived in the city, there were still parts of Roman society protocol that my grandmother understood far better than I ever would.

Our business trade continued to prosper. By this point, Uncle Linus considered me a full partner in our dye and linen business. Very few decisions were made without my being consulted. Linus said he was keeping my father apprised of my progress throughout my time in Rome.

A few weeks before Lucius and I were to be married, Linus confided in me, "I have told your father we would be foolish to exclude you from the management of the business. You understand it as well, if not better, than we do. Plus, you have a gift for negotiating the best price while leaving our customers and suppliers with a smile on their faces."

Then he added with a laugh, "I told your father if Lucius didn't ask you to marry him, I was going to – so we would be assured of your continued involvement in the business!"

Lucius knew how his father felt and told me he completely agreed. He was not threatened by my ability; rather, he felt our talents complemented one another – and I thought so too!

There was an uproar in Rome exactly one month before our wedding. Uncle Aurelius had been reporting for some time that the senate was receiving mixed messages from Emperor Tiberius about his confidence in Prefect Sejanus. Supporters were beginning to take sides and declare their allegiance. The senate was waiting to see how the emperor would respond.

On October 18, Sejanus was summoned to a senate meeting by a letter from the emperor, allegedly to grant him additional powers. However, Uncle Aurelius told us that afternoon, "Sejanus entered the senate hall at first light as a directive from the emperor was being read aloud. The letter addressed routine matters of business and Sejanus, as well as other members of the senate, anxiously awaited the announcement. But suddenly the letter took an unexpected turn. Tiberius denounced Sejanus and ordered he be arrested immediately and executed for treason against the emperor."

I couldn't help but feel sad for Sejanus. I would never know if he was really making treasonous plans, but I knew he had been the tragic victim of his own selfish ambition. I silently said a word of thanks to the gods for protecting me from being in the middle of that sadness and tragedy.

There was one element of personal sadness, however, that surrounded my wedding. Three weeks prior to the day of our celebration, I received a letter from my father which read:

My dearest Lydia,

Ever since the news of your engagement, your mother and I have looked forward to joining you in Rome for the occasion of your wedding. Please know how much we would have relished being there with you and Lucius to celebrate your special day. But, alas, circumstances have arisen that will prevent us from doing so.

Do not be alarmed, but my physicians have diagnosed me with an illness called "phthisis." It is characterized by prolonged episodes of fever and fitful coughing. They have advised me that a long journey would not be in my best interest at this time. They continue to confine me to my bed and treat me with their remedies. They assure me that if I follow their advice the illness will pass.

It is not something that you need to be concerned about. I will get better. But it has come at a very inconvenient time. I have encouraged your mother to come to Rome without me, but she is refusing to do so. So, regrettably we will need to celebrate with you from afar. Please know that our thoughts and hearts are with you, and please do not allow our absence to cast a shadow on your special day.

With all my love,

Your father

In my father's absence, Uncle Linus did me the honor of giving me away to marry Lucius. Despite my parents' absence, it was a joyful day. The arrangements, all handled by my grandmother down to the smallest details, were perfect. She again remarked it was one of the social events of the year in Rome. But that honestly didn't make much difference to me. All I cared about was marrying the one with whom I wanted to spend the rest of my life!

That day I moved out of the palatial dwelling that had been my home for the past six years – now the home of Uncle Aurelius and Aunt Diana. I moved into the more modest home of a successful merchant and tradesman with my husband. In many ways, this house felt more like home, and I waved goodbye to the provincial girl of my past.

My father and mother continued to write that my father's health was improving, and they assured me there was no reason for me to return to Thyatira. However, tragedy soon struck right there in Rome. The year following my marriage, my grandmother was struck with a fever that passed through the city. Aunt Diana and I did all we could to nurse her and keep her comfortable. But nothing the physicians did was able to change the course of her fever. Ten days after falling ill, she died.

Her funeral was much less grand than my grandfather's. We buried the urn with her ashes beside those of my grandfather. I missed them both, and I would often walk to the cemetery and stand by their monument and talk to them. Somehow, I felt they were both still giving me good counsel – even from the grave.

Though I was grateful for the family around me – Lucius, Linus, Aurelius, Diana, and Pudens – I found myself missing my family in Thyatira. Rome no longer felt quite the same without my grandparents. For the first time in six years, I considered returning to Thyatira. I believed my time in Rome may soon be drawing to an end.

One morning I awakened to the news that the day of my return had arrived. My father had died. His condition had worsened – apparently at an alarming rate. My mother needed me … and truth be told, I needed her. Uncle Linus agreed that Lucius and I needed to go. We needed to comfort my family, but we also needed to tend to business affairs in Thyatira. He would keep everything running smoothly in Rome, but my brother would need our help in Thyatira.

Lucius made our travel arrangements, and we said goodbye to our family and friends in Rome not knowing when, or if, we would see them again. My voyage to Rome years ago had been exciting, but this trip was filled with sadness. I was despondent about leaving Rome, but I was absolutely heartbroken to return to a Thyatira that no longer included my father.

10

THE SURPRISE THAT AWAITED ME

~

*I*t took us two weeks to sail from Rome to Miletus, then another six days to make our way overland to Thyatira. As we stood on the hill overlooking the city, I was surprised that it looked much smaller than I remembered. I also missed seeing the grand buildings I had grown so accustomed to in Rome. But the hills surrounding the city were still as lush and beautiful as I remembered them.

We arrived at my parents' home just before nightfall. There was a part of me that hoped the message I had received was all a mistake – and my father would be there to greet me at the door. But that was not the case; my mother opened the door.

She looked worn and tired. I had never seen her like this. My father's illness and death had taken a great toll on her. She clung to me in a welcoming embrace, but it was more than just joy and relief to see us; she needed to draw from my strength.

Janus came into the room a few minutes later. My eighteen-year-old brother was now quite the man, looking ever so much like our father. But he too looked haggard, as if the weight of the world now rested on his shoulders.

The servants prepared a meal, and Lucius and I gratefully ate since we were hungry from our journey. But I noticed my mother and brother ate very little. I quickly realized the confident mother I had last seen in Rome was now completely overwrought with grief. Janus wasn't in much better shape. He was now the man of the house and the leader of our family business. However, the first was a position he wasn't ready for; the second was a role he never wanted.

I knew they both needed me to be strong right now – to help them walk through their grief and to navigate all the responsibilities they were facing. That night, Lucius and I listened as they expressed their pain, and we all cried together. We would talk about next steps later, but for now they needed to release the sorrow they had been holding in.

None of us got much sleep that night, but the glimmer of dawn reminded us that no matter how dark things may be, the sun will always rise to help us find the way. I suggested we all rest for a few hours. Then Janus and I would go to the family's place of business later in the morning. Lucius stayed with my mother and brightened her spirits with stories about Rome.

I had always known my father was an excellent salesman. Uncle Linus was always quick to remind me no one could outsell my father – but then he would add, "except you." But Linus had also confided that my father did not watch costs as closely as he should. That was one of the talents Linus contributed to their partnership. But their physical distance apart kept Linus from monitoring the business in Thyatira as closely as was needed.

Our business in Thyatira always appeared to be thriving because my father was very adept at borrowing money and enlisting new investors. Those funds offset the losses my father was actually incurring. Somehow, he had been able to juggle it all. But now that he was gone, the lenders and investors did not have that same confidence in my brother. They were demanding immediate payment, and as Janus told me, "There is no money with which to pay them!" My father had been deep in debt, and now the responsibility fell to us to pay off that debt.

Gratefully, I had not only acquired my father's sales ability, but I had also been an attentive student of my Uncle Linus. I knew we could make the business as profitable as the one in Rome; all it required was time. And it was up to me to convince the lenders and investors to give us that time.

Most of the men my father dealt with would remember me as the adorable little girl who followed in her father's shadow. So, I knew it would be hard for them to see me as a capable young businesswoman. I needed to assure them that the three of us – my brother, my husband, and I – were capable of providing them with the income they had expected to receive from my father. It would require every ounce of my sales ability.

I sent an invitation to the lenders and investors from Janus, Lucius, and me that read, "Please honor us with your presence at our place of business two weeks from today, at which time we will outline how you will be repaid the capital you entrusted to our father, together with the income your trust in him has yielded." Though I had no idea what the plan was going to be, I had at least given myself a two-week reprieve.

I dispatched Janus to work with the dye makers; he had always demonstrated an affinity for that part of the business. I was confident he would discover ways of reducing our costs without sacrificing quality – needed changes I knew my father had always resisted. Lucius had spent a lot of time in the linen shops in Rome. I tasked him with the responsibility of reducing our costs in that area. And I started meeting with our main patrons to convince them why our products were worth an increase in price.

By the end of the two-week period, we had increased our profit margins substantially and were able to present a plan to our investors and lenders that would repay them in two years' time with a handsome profit as well. They were so impressed with our work they unanimously agreed – and I don't think any of them saw me as that adorable little girl walking in her father's shadow any longer.

11

A LIFE IS GIVEN, AND A LIFE IS TAKEN

~

*A*s the weeks passed, my mother's countenance began to brighten. She took strength from having all of us around her. And though we had never bothered her with business concerns, she could tell things had improved. She sensed Janus's relief and his confidence in me to provide the necessary leadership.

It surprised me that I was no longer homesick for Rome. I was gradually embracing Thyatira as the home I once held close to my heart, and I was thriving in the opportunity to lead our business. However, I was painfully aware that it was still a man's world. Representatives from the guild invited Janus and Lucius to take the seat vacated by my father; they never considered inviting me. But for now, I tried to be content with the progress we had made.

One week later, those concerns were set aside when I realized I was expecting my first child. The news of the baby breathed even more life into our home and family. Somehow the skies continued to brighten.

The favorite topic at every family gathering after that was whether Lucius's and my child would be a boy or a girl. Lucius and Janus were hoping for a boy. My mother vacillated –some days she wanted a boy, other days a girl. But I never wavered. I was trusting the gods for a daughter. I prided myself on having a strength of character I had inherited from my mother, and she had inherited from her mother. I wanted the opportunity to pass that strength on to my daughter.

The day of the baby's arrival came quickly for some, but I will confess it seemed much longer for me. As the months passed, I developed a greater appreciation for all my mother had gone through to bring me into the world. It doesn't matter how much your mother shares with you, you never really understand until you experience it for yourself!

I had just returned home from meeting with one of our patrons when I knew the time had come. I sent our servant, Sergius, to get the midwife as his wife, Oppia, and my mother helped me prepare. I knew Lucius would be of no help at this point, so I suggested he go for a long walk. My labor continued throughout the night and into the next morning. But finally, I was rewarded with the cries of . . . a baby girl.

"What will you name her?" my mother asked.

"We will name her Valeria," I answered. "Because she will grow up to be brave and strong."

"Just like her mother," my mother smiled through tears of joy. I knew she was wishing my father were here to witness the birth of his first grandchild.

Valeria lived up to her name from the time she was a little girl, demonstrating the same strength of character I had shown at her age. Lucius and I made sure she had a quality education. We hired some of the finest tutors, and when we discovered there were subjects for which experienced teachers were not available, Lucius, my mother, or I taught her. By the time she was ten, she had spent many afternoons with me at our place of business.

Our family business continued to thrive, and we had now expanded our trade into Macedonia. My father would have been proud! We were discussing the possibility of sending a representative to the city of Philippi, which would open up additional opportunities in Macedonia as well as in Thrace. Several of our former investors were pleading with me for the opportunity to invest in our expansion.

It was gratifying that the guild and investors finally acknowledged I was the one running the business. They no longer went to Lucius and Janus to discuss such matters. My husband and brother still held the seat in the guild, but I expected that too would soon change.

Lucius and I had been planning a trip to Rome to visit family. Linus had come to Thyatira for a visit a few years after Valeria was born. He said he came to discuss important business matters, but we all knew he had come to meet his granddaughter! Now another ten years had passed, and we longed for our daughter to spend more time with her grandfather and experience the great city.

A few days before we were to leave on the journey, a fever passed through our city. Lucius, Valeria, and Janus all came down with it. Gratefully, my mother and I escaped it, so we were able to care for the others. The midwife showed us how to prepare and apply the poultice being used to treat those with fever.

Valeria and Janus began to improve after several days and gradually regained their strength. But Lucius was showing no signs of improvement. I spoke to the midwife about trying a different treatment, but she told me there was nothing more she knew to do. I had never been a deeply religious woman, but I even called out to the gods to heal my husband. But those cries proved to be no more effective than the poultice.

On the ninth day of his fever, Lucius died. Though I had walked through the pain with my mother and grandmother when they lost their husbands, I realized you cannot truly understand how it feels to lose a spouse until you experience that grief yourself. Thankfully, my mother was there to help me through every step of my journey.

I've never told this to anyone, but I sometimes wonder if I would have made it through had my mother not been right beside me. Yes, I had my daughter to think about. She had just lost her father – much too soon. She needed me, and I needed to be strong for her. But truthfully, I had no strength left in me . . . and I had no gods to call upon.

I relied heavily on my mother's strength to make it out of that valley. And while I didn't realize it at the time, it was my husband's death that set me on a mission to find the true meaning of life. What was the purpose of life amid all this pain and death? I'd lost Lucius. I'd almost lost Valeria. The purpose had to be more than live well and die. And it most certainly wasn't the dye and cloth business!

~

<h1 style="text-align:center">12</h1>

SEARCHING FOR THE UNKNOWN

~

Without Lucius to help shoulder the responsibility, I had to assume his duties of managing the linen shops. I worked hard and in time increased the number of shops under our management. Having already been recognized as the manufacturer of the highest-quality dye, we were now also recognized as the largest supplier of dyed linen in Thyatira. Our business had never been better.

The guild could no longer ignore my accomplishments. They risked angering the patrons with their prejudicial disrespect. Reluctantly, they granted me a seat on the guild despite the reservations voiced by several longtime members. My only regret the day the seat was awarded to me was that my father and husband were not there to witness it. But I knew they both would have been proud of my accomplishment.

Looking back, I realize my increased workload was my way of masking the pain of losing Lucius. But in doing so, I robbed Valeria of the mother she needed. I am so thankful my mother was there to fill that void; but, nonetheless, I was wrong in what I did. The worst part is it cost me precious time with my daughter that I will never get back.

Around that time, I met a woman about my age named Rebecca. She also was an eldest daughter working for her father. He had established one of the successful linen shops we had recently acquired, but I quickly determined *she* was the primary reason for the shop's success. Her gender prevented her from receiving the recognition she deserved. But I planned to change that!

The more I got to know Rebecca, the more I admired her character. Since Lucius's death, I had become more interested in pursuing spiritual ideas. I quickly decided the Roman gods held no interest for me; they were simply imaginative stories. And the sun god, Apollo, who is so prominent in our city, held no place in my heart.

One day I asked Rebecca what she believed, and she began to tell me about the God of the Jews. Instead of a plethora of self-centered gods, she told me how her people, the Israelites, had been chosen by One called Jehovah God to be His people.

"The God of our patriarchs delivered us from slavery at the hands of our Egyptian taskmasters over 1,500 years ago and eventually led us to a land He promised to give us," she told me. "Our people prospered under His hand until we were taken captive by the Assyrians and Babylonians due to our disobedience to Him."

As she explained more about Him, I began to understand He was a just and compassionate God – not fickle – but true to His word. The more she spoke about Him, the more curious I became. I wasn't ready to join her in worship, but I could not get this God out of my mind.

As the months passed, I assigned additional responsibility to Rebecca. I was confident she could lead our other linen shops to become even more efficient. I was right! Within months, we were able to seek out additional patrons because of our increased production capability.

Janus and I decided we needed to make her a partner in our business. That action led to two important life changes for me. Though Valeria was with me most afternoons at the business, I still spent very little quality time with her. So, I decided to reduce my work hours and instead plan more mother-daughter activities with Valeria. She was approaching her sixteenth birthday, and I knew our remaining days would pass quickly.

I was mindful of the time my mother and I had spent together in Rome when I was Valeria's age. Those years had made an indelible impression on my life. That prompted me to consider doing the same with Valeria. It would give her time with her grandfather, Linus, and Uncle Aurelius, as well as an education that would be unmatched. But I could not find peace with the decision. Even my mother counseled me to consider an alternate plan.

That is when the idea for the second big change began to form. Our Roman heritage had always influenced our lives, but I also knew our Macedonian blood had helped shape us. I could hear my father's words playing over and over again in my head: "Lydia, Macedonian blood flows through your veins. Be true to your heritage and honor your Macedonian forefathers."

Our heritage was drawing me to take my daughter to Macedonia. But there was also a business opportunity there. Janus and Rebecca were quite capable of overseeing our business operations in Thyatira just as Linus was doing in Rome. This would be an opportunity to expand our business into Macedonia – and in many ways, to return to the place where it all started. And who better to do that than Valeria and me?

When I shared the idea with my mother, she agreed. "Your father would be so proud of you. You would be doing something he always wanted to do. In many ways, you and Valeria would be helping him achieve an unfulfilled dream. You should do it, Lydia! You will never know what could come from your time there if you don't."

"Should I return to the homeplace of our ancestors, the city of Pella?" I asked, not really expecting an answer.

"No," my mother replied. "Go to the city of Philippi. It is the new gateway to Macedonia."

I knew the moment she spoke those words I was to go there – but I had no idea why my heart had such certainty!

13

MY ARRIVAL IN PHILIPPI

≈

Two months later, Valeria and I – together with our two servants, Sergius and Oppia – set out for Philippi. We traveled overland to Smyrna where we boarded a riverboat that navigated along the coast to Troas. After resting there overnight, we boarded the ferry and crossed the northern tip of the Aegean Sea landing at the island of Samothrace. The next day we continued on the rest of our journey and arrived at the harbor of Neapolis. It took us nine days to make the journey from Thyatira to the coast of Macedonia.

The minute we arrived in the harbor we knew we had stepped into a different world – it was a true mixture of diverse cultures. The port and surrounding towns were originally established by my Macedonian ancestors about 400 years earlier to mine gold. Soldiers had been assigned to several garrisons to protect the mining operations. One of those forts, situated sixteen kilometers inland from Neapolis, was the town of Philippi, named in honor of King Philip II, the father of Alexander the Great. For 200 years, it served as a strategic military outpost.

But that all changed when Macedonia came under Roman rule. One of Rome's massive accomplishments soon after conquering the region was the construction of the Via Egnatia, a highway built on the backs of slave labor that stretched almost 800 kilometers (nearly 500 miles) from the Adriatic Sea to the Aegean Sea. It created an efficient trade route on which to move soldiers and goods by land from Italy to Asia and back again.

Located at its eastern end, Philippi became a gateway center – politically, commercially, militarily, and culturally. The city was redeveloped using a pattern similar to that of Rome and was colonized by veteran soldiers, many of whom were from the elite Praetorian guard. Other Roman citizens seeking opportunity and good fortune also flocked to the city, and its borders eventually extended to Neapolis.

My first order of business was to introduce myself to the local Roman magistrate. I knew that a woman with a small entourage planning to take up residence and establish a business in the city – all without a man – would raise questions. I wanted to answer them before they even arose.

The ferry captain had explained to me the city magistrate was in fact two military officers who had been appointed to be the duumviri (the co-magistrates responsible for governing the city). Officers Camillus and Marcellus, the duumviri of Philippi, were easy to locate; they resided in a large home that overlooked the entire city. I found out they had been assigned to their positions by the Roman senate a little more than two years earlier.

When I first began speaking with the men, they showed little interest in me and even less courtesy. So I decided to get their attention. "Your honors," I began, "I am a merchant of purple cloth from the city of Thyatira seeking to expand our trade into this region. My father's ances-tors are from this part of the world, whereas my mother is part of an important family in Rome. You may have heard of her deceased father and my grandfather, Senator Gaius, as well as my uncle, Senator Aurelius."

Both men immediately gave me their full attention. "Yes, we are very familiar with your grandfather and your uncle," Camillus, the older of the two, replied. "In fact, your uncle presented our credentials before the senate just two years ago so we might be appointed to this office. We are in his debt."

Marcellus nodded. "Yes, we wholeheartedly welcome you to our city. We are honored that someone of your station has chosen to come here. But we must ask, given the business you plan to establish here, will your husband be joining you?"

"No, I'm afraid not," I replied. "Sadly, he passed away almost three years ago. Today I run our business. My grandfather always taught me to apply myself. I work in partnership with my brother, who manages our operations in Thyatira, and a good family friend who manages the business in Rome on the Vicus Sobrius, which as you know houses only the finest businesses of the city." The two men were now practically standing at attention.

"I would appreciate your assistance in finding accommodations that are commensurate with my station for both my daughter and me, as well as my servants," I continued. "And I will need to find a suitable place to conduct my trade in the better part of your business district. In the meantime, where might you recommend we lodge for the evening?"

After that, I wanted for nothing. The duumviri were most attentive to my every need. That evening we stayed in their guest quarters, and the following day we moved into our new home situated on the hill overlooking the city. Once settled, I began to explore the three locations the duumviri suggested might be suitable for my business.

When I entered the second location – and what proved to be the last in my search – I was greeted by a young woman named Naomi. It was a linen shop that appeared to be successfully catering to an elite clientele in the city. From the first moment, I was impressed with Naomi's demeanor. Her father owned the business, but it only took moments to realize she was running it. I could not get over how much she reminded me of Rebecca – her manner, her competence, and her character.

After we talked about business for a while, I changed the subject. "Are you a follower of Jehovah God? Are you a Jew?"

"Yes, I am," she replied. "I am surprised you would ask if I am a Jew. Very few people in our city know about the Jews; there are only a handful of us here. Why do you ask?"

"Because a good friend of mine in Thyatira is Jewish," I answered, "and she has begun to teach me about your beliefs. She told me to find the synagogue when I arrived here in Philippi."

"We don't yet have a synagogue in this city since there aren't enough of us," Naomi explained. "In our religion there must be ten men in order to establish a synagogue, and of our few number most are women. We gather by the river each Sabbath to pray. You are welcome to join us."

"I may do just that," I told her. "Besides, you and I will be spending a lot of time together. I intend to buy your business – so very soon you will be working for me."

～

14

GATHERING FOR PRAYER

～

There is no question that the city of Philippi has prospered under the influence of Rome. Though the city is surrounded by Macedonian-era walls, vestiges of Roman life have slowly been added to its interior. A forum, or public marketplace, is situated on either side of the main road. It is the center of daily life and houses some of the most prestigious enterprises of the city, including mine. A large theater has also been built for the city's chief entertainment – the Roman games.

On the next Sabbath day, I joined Naomi and four other women along the river as they gathered to pray. I learned that one of the women was also not Jewish. She had been seeking the one true God and had been drawn to the God of the Jews. With the arrival of Valeria, my two servants, and me, we nearly doubled the size of the gathering.

Naomi and the other women took turns reading aloud from their holy book, the Torah. That day they were reading words written by a prophet named Isaiah. After a while, they invited me to read these words:

"The Spirit of the Sovereign Lord is upon Me,
for the Lord has anointed Me
to bring good news to the poor.
He has sent Me to comfort the brokenhearted
and to proclaim that captives will be released
and prisoners will be freed.
He has sent Me to tell those who mourn
that the time of the Lord's favor has come,
and with it, the day of God's anger against their enemies.
To all who mourn in Israel,
He will give a crown of beauty for ashes,
a joyous blessing instead of mourning,
festive praise instead of despair.
In their righteousness, they will be like great oaks
that the Lord has planted for His own glory."[1]

No god I had ever heard of promised to exchange beauty for ashes, blessing for mourning, or praise for despair. Every other god I knew about had always wanted something from me. My desire to know this God of the Jews increased.

The other women began to praise their God, speaking these words in unison:

"I prayed to the Lord, and He answered me.
He freed me from all my fears.
Those who look to Him for help will be radiant with joy;
no shadow of shame will darken their faces.
In my desperation I prayed, and the Lord listened;
He saved me from all my troubles.
For the angel of the Lord is a guard;
He surrounds and defends all who fear Him.[2]

I looked at Valeria, Sergius, and Oppia; tears were streaming down their faces. None of us could describe what was happening, but I sensed a presence I had never felt before. We continued to read and pray throughout the morning – and I didn't want our time to end.

But when it was over, I knew I would return to that place and join those women every week; Valeria and my servants felt the same. The next words in that psalm spoke to me as well:

> *Taste and see that the Lord is good.*
> *Oh, the joys of those who take refuge in Him!*[3]

That's exactly what I wanted to do. I had tasted of His goodness and I wanted to know Him more – His peace, His love, His mercy. The rest of that day and in the days that followed, I continued to hear those words in my mind.

My business in Philippi was flourishing. The purple dye was now arriving regularly from Thyatira on the merchant ships, and we had three linen shops producing our cloth for dyeing. With Naomi overseeing our production in Philippi, I was able to travel to other cities along the Via Egnatia, including Berea and Thessalonica.

Demand for our product increased everywhere I visited once buyers heard that these were the fabrics being worn by the elite of Rome. Ours were becoming the most sought-after fabrics of Macedonia, just as they were throughout Asia and Italy.

Though Valeria was not receiving the Roman education I had hoped for her, she was blossoming as she traveled to different places and experienced a diversity of cultures. Her father would have said she was becoming just like me – and he would have been right! I knew Lucius would be so proud if he could see the young lady she was now.

One day as we were returning to Philippi, Valeria asked, "Mother, we have lived in Macedonia for almost a year. Do you believe we will remain here, or do you think we will move elsewhere?"

"Why do you ask?" I inquired.

"Because I do not want to live anywhere else! I like the sights, the sounds, the sea, and the people. I particularly like Naomi, and our other friends, and our weekly gatherings at the riverbank on the Sabbath. I like the way it makes me feel. It has helped me work through the pain of Daddy's death. I'm not sure if it's the gathering or Jehovah God who has made me feel better. Maybe it's both. All I know is I don't want to leave. I want to stay here and bask in the way it makes me feel."

"So do I, Valeria," I said, as I pondered her words. I couldn't have said it better myself! I had tasted and seen that the Lord is good, and I didn't want to risk losing that feeling.

~

15

AN UNEXPECTED VISITOR AT THE RIVER

∾

One Sabbath day, as everyone in my household was walking to the riverbank, we were approached by a girl at least four or five years younger than Valeria.

"Matron, may I tell you your fortune?" she asked, as she stared at me with a curious expression. "I am able to tell you what will happen in your life – love that will be gained, love that will be lost, fortune that will be gained, and the like. All you have to do is ask me and give me a few coins. I have much I can tell you about yourself."

"I fear there is little you can tell me that I don't already know, my girl," I answered. I saw two men leaning against a tree nearby who were listening to our every word and watching our every move. "But I also fear these men may be taking advantage of you," I said as I looked at the two men. "What is your name, girl?"

"They call me Rumena, matron," the girl replied, "and no, these men do not take advantage of me; they take good care of me and treat me well. I couldn't ask for better, and I know it to be so because I've looked into my future. How about you? Can I tell you what I see in your future?"

"No, Rumena," I responded. "I am not in the habit of giving my coins to line the pockets of men who take advantage of young girls. But if you ever need someone to help you when you are free of their bondage, you come see me."

Then I called out to the men, "And you see that you take good care of her and bring her no harm. Or I will see that you feel the full sting of Roman justice across your backs!"

Both men waved me off and turned their heads, but I knew they had heard me – and knew I was true to my word. After all, the whole city now knew me as the wealthy woman who lives on the hill next to the duumviri.

As we continued to the river, I turned back to Rumena and said, "We are going to the bank of the river to sing and pray to Jehovah God. Would you like to join us?"

She looked at the men and then back to me as she answered, "No, matron, I cannot worship Jehovah God. But thank you for your kindness. And if I ever need a hand, I will come see you."

As we set off, she whispered to me, "You will meet a man there today who will answer all your questions."

I do not believe in fortunetelling so I did not take her words to heart, but I could not get the girl out of mind. She was being used by those men – and though I knew legally she was their property – I couldn't help but ponder how I might rescue her from her life of bondage.

When we arrived at the riverbank, Naomi and the other women were already there. But we were surprised to see four men whom I did not recognize speaking with them. One of the men – slightly older than I am and small of stature – was doing most of the talking. He was introduced to us as Paul from the town of Tarsus.

The other three were his traveling companions. The oldest was a physician named Luke who told us he was from Antioch in Syria. He was the quietest of the four and seemed intent on listening to everything being said. The third man, Silas, was about my age and originally from Alexandria. He told me he had been traveling with Paul for about two years.

Timothy was the youngest of the four and about the age of my cousin, Pudens, but he looked even younger. He was from Lystra and was apparently being mentored by Paul.

The men had just arrived in Macedonia. Paul and Silas had begun their journey in Antioch and the other two had joined them along the way. It soon became obvious that Paul was a learned teacher and preacher.

As we read from the Torah together, Paul opened it to the same writing in Isaiah that I had read on my first Sabbath with the women. The words warmed my heart just as they had before. I had seen how Jehovah God could bring joy where there was mourning and praise where there had been despair.

Paul went on to tell us that the One sent by Jehovah God to set the captives free was named Jesus – the Promised One. He came to earth to be born of a virgin and live a righteous life without sin. His blood was shed on a cross as the covering for our sin. God had come to earth in the person of Jesus to set us free.

Because of His sacrifice on the cross, our mourning and despair could be wiped away – our sins forgiven. But Paul told us Jesus had not remained in the grave after His crucifixion. If He had, we would have had no hope! Rather, He arose from the grave on the third day. He is not a dead sacrifice . . . He is a living Savior!

The more Paul spoke, the more my heart leapt. I knew this was the truth. My spirit within me bore witness. So I asked Paul, "What must I do to be saved?"

He replied, *"Repent of your sins and turn to God, and be baptized in the name of Jesus Christ for the forgiveness of your sins. And you will receive the gift of the Holy Spirit. This promise is to you, to your children, and to those far away — all who have been called by the Lord our God."*[1]

As I listened, the Lord opened my heart and made it clear what I should do next.

∼

16

COME AND STAY AT MY HOME

∼

I knew I must be baptized. We were already on the bank of the river; there would never be a better time. I called out to Paul, "I do repent, and I believe in the name of Jesus. Will you baptize me?"

The next voice I heard, though, was not Paul's – it was Valeria's. "I also repent and believe. And I, too, want to be baptized in the name of Jesus!" I turned to my daughter and we embraced. Within moments, Sergius and Oppia spoke the same confession. All four of us stood there with our arms wrapped around one another, tears of joy streaming down our faces.

With the other men and women as witnesses, Paul baptized the four of us. The other women weren't quite sure what they should do. They did not take their step of belief that day – though each would do so in the days to come.

Once we were standing back on dry land, I asked Paul, "Do you and your companions have a place to stay here in Philippi?"

"God has provided us with a room for the past several nights," he replied.

I felt prompted to invite them to stay in my home. *"If you agree that I am faithful to the Lord,"* I said, *"come and stay at my home."*[1]

I knew it was highly unusual for an unmarried woman to extend such an invitation to four men, but I felt compelled to do so. I believed the Lord had plans for my home that extended beyond simple lodging. Apparently, so did Paul, because after a few moments he accepted my invitation.

Later that day as we ate a meal together, he recounted the journey that had brought them to Philippi.

"After staying with Timothy and his parents for a while, I received their permission to bring him along on a journey I thought would take us only as far as those cities of Asia immediately surrounding Lystra. I had given them assurances we would travel no farther," Paul said. "But those plans had not included the redirection we subsequently received from the Holy Spirit!

"As we approached the cities on the western border of Phrygia, Silas and I were restrained from entering them by the Spirit of the Lord. Rather, He directed us to turn northward and go toward the provinces of Bithynia and Pontus. Though I had not visited those regions, Timothy told us some believers from Iconium had been there to share the Good News. This path would allow us to preach and encourage the believers in those cities – or so I thought.

"But, as we approached that border, the Spirit again redirected us and turned us back toward the west. He again restrained us from entering the cities along the way – including your home of Thyatira. Instead, we found ourselves in the seaport town of Troas on the eastern shore of the Aegean Sea. When we had set out from Antioch, I never envisioned God would lead us there. But obviously He had other plans.

"Our next surprise was when we encountered Luke on the streets of Troas not long after we arrived. 'Shortly after the two of you left Antioch,' he told us, 'the Spirit of the Lord came to me in a dream and told me to come to Troas.' Luke had asked Him, 'For what purpose?' And the Spirit of the Lord had responded, 'I will show you once you get there.'

"Luke questioned whether or not it was really the Lord. But when the Lord directed him a second time, he knew he must act quickly. He arrived in Troas the very morning that Silas, Timothy, and I arrived."

Paul continued, "That night, I had a vision. I saw a man from Macedonia pleading with me, saying, '*Come over here and help us.*'[2] The next morning, I shared my dream with the other men. We all agreed there was no question what God was directing us to do next!

"We boarded a ferry that day and set sail to the harbor of Neapolis. That was four days ago. Today the Spirit of the Lord allowed me to see that the man standing on the shore in my vision was really a group of women praying by the riverbank. The Spirit of the Lord was at work in this place long before we ever set foot on this shore – and what He begins, He will complete!" Paul concluded.

As a new follower of Jesus, I had much to learn and absorb. But it didn't take long before I was taught a painful lesson – the devil does not like his territory invaded.

The day after Paul baptized me, I traveled to Amphipolis on business and took Valeria with me. I told Paul and his companions to make themselves comfortable in my home, and I charged my servants with attending to their needs.

Paul decided to return each morning to the riverbank to teach about Jesus to those who gathered. The crowds grew larger day after day. On the second day, Paul and Silas noticed a young girl following them on the path. They didn't know her, but it was Rumena. As she walked behind them, she began to shout, *"These men are servants of the Most High God, and they have come to tell you how to be saved."*[3]

This continued for several days until Paul became so exasperated by the distraction he finally spoke up. He had known from the first day it was not Rumena talking but the demon who had control over her. He addressed the demon directly: *"I command you in the name of Jesus Christ to come out of her!"*[4] Instantly it left her – and immediately her shouting stopped.

Paul and Silas continued on their way to the riverbank and began to teach. But it didn't take long for her masters to discover that Rumena's ability to tell fortunes left with the demon – and their hopes of wealth with it. When the two men realized what had happened, they cast her aside and set out to find Paul and Silas.

～

17

WRONGFULLY PUNISHED

~

*M*ost of the townspeople in Philippi were wary of the Jews. They knew Jewish people believed in only one God – which was contrary to their own beliefs. A large number of the residents did not want the Jews living in their city.

But since there were so few Jews, the duumviri had decided they were not a threat. A majority of the people accepted that decision, but there remained a few who would never be trusting or accepting. Rumena's masters knew this smaller group could easily be swayed to attack the Jews and stir the greater population into turmoil.

Within an hour, the two men had worked a small mob into a frenzy, which they then led to the riverbank where Paul and Silas were teaching. The mob grabbed Paul and Silas and dragged them to the center of the forum shouting, *"The whole city is in an uproar because of these Jews. They are teaching customs that are illegal for us Romans to practice."*[1]

If I had been there, I could have spoken on their behalf and calmed the crowd. But God in His sovereignty chose for me to be away from the city. The gathering began to grow even larger. Camillus and Marcellus were summoned to address the matter and rule on what needed to be done to Paul and Silas.

In light of their own religious and racial prejudices, the duumviri did not listen to any defense from Paul or Silas. Instead, they assessed the overwhelming accusations of the crowd and decided to follow their lead. They ordered Paul and Silas to be stripped and beaten. The fact the two men were Roman citizens should have prevented that action, but the duumviri never bothered to ask the question – and they never allowed Paul or Silas to speak. Instead, they ordered the city jailer to severely beat them with wooden rods and lock them in prison. The jailer, on his part, took no chances. He locked them in the inner dungeon and clamped their feet in stocks.

Paul and Silas were wrongfully accused, wrongfully judged, and wrongfully punished. Despite that, Paul later told me, "As we sat in the dungeon, an overwhelming peace came over us – a peace that could only be explained by the presence of the Holy Spirit. Our heads told us we should shout at the top of our lungs with pleas of innocence and injustice, but our spirits told us to lift our voices to God with praises and hymns.

"Around midnight, as the other prisoners were listening to us praying and singing, a great earthquake shook the very foundation of the prison. All the doors flew open, and the chains of every prisoner fell off. Although the prisoners could have fled to freedom, they remained right where they were. They sat there in awe of God, which overshadowed any fear they had of our Roman captors. I don't know with complete certainty, but I believe a number of our fellow prisoners came to faith in Jesus that night.

"My attention was fixed on the jailer. Roman law demands that if a jailer loses a prisoner, he will receive the same punishment as the prisoner. Several of the men imprisoned were facing severe punishments. When the jailer saw the doors were open and feared the prisoners had escaped, he knew the penalty he would face. I watched as he drew his sword to kill himself.

"It would have been easy to justify taking vengeance on our persecutor by allowing him to take his own life. But I knew the jailer was really the prisoner – imprisoned by his own sin. Silas and I were truly freed men – set free from the bondage of sin. I knew I was no more worthy of the grace extended to me through the compassion of Christ than this cruel jailer. So, I shouted out, '*Don't kill yourself! We are all here!*'[2]

"The power of God is what had seized the jailer's attention, but it was the grace and compassion of God that made him understand his need for a Savior. It wasn't the supernatural power of the earthquake that God used to draw this man to Himself; it was a spirit of humility, grace, and kindness that drew him to the Gospel.

"Trembling with fear, the jailer, whose name we learned is Aeropos, asked us, '*Sirs, what must I do to be saved?*'[3] That night, he and all the members of his household heard the Good News, believed, and were baptized. An evening that started with Aeropos subjecting us to severe beatings ended with him washing our wounds and extending us hospitality," Paul concluded.

Valeria and I arrived back in Philippi late that night. Early the next morning, Timothy and Luke reported to me what had happened. They told me Paul and Silas were wrongfully imprisoned; I feared for what had happened to them.

I immediately sought out Camillus and Marcellus. "Do you men know what you have done?" I asked as soon as I entered their hall.

"About what?" they asked, startled by my tone.

"You have ordered that two of the guests living in my home be beaten and imprisoned! Not only have you greatly offended me, but you also have violated the law of the empire by subjecting Roman citizens to illegal treatment! By law, you are required to have given them a fair trial – not punish them at the whim of an angry mob. Believe me when I say, the senate will hear of your offenses!"

The two men looked at one another in fear. Camillus stuttered, "But the witnesses accused them of inciting a riot, and the crowd bore further witness."

"So you took the word of the men who have oppressed that young girl as their slave over the word of two men who are guests in my home?" I demanded. "And you have allowed the very people you told to set aside their prejudices against the Jews to now sway your opinion?

"I can assure you my uncle would never condone the action you have taken. Apparently, his trust has been greatly misplaced in you! I will be sending word to him immediately!"

Camillus and Marcellus looked at one another in fear. "Our honorable patrician, that will not be necessary," Marcellus insisted. "Obviously, a grave error has occurred. Thank you for bringing it to our attention. We relied upon testimony that we now know to be false. We will immediately set it right by sending word for the prisoners to be released."

∼

18

A CHURCH IS BORN

~

The soldiers dispatched by the duumviri soon arrived at the jail with this message, *"Let those men go!"* [1]

Aeropos later told me that he was overjoyed to receive the news. He had been considering a way to release Paul and Silas without endangering his family or himself. So he happily entered the jail to announce to Paul, *"The city officials have said you and Silas are free to leave. Go in peace."* [2]

But he was shocked when Paul replied, *"They have publicly beaten us without a trial and put us in prison – and we are Roman citizens. So now they want us to leave secretly? Certainly not! Let them come themselves to release us!"* [3]

When the soldiers reported back to the duumviri that Paul and Silas were refusing to leave, Camillus and Marcellus again became frightened about what would happen to them if news about this made its way to Rome. Would I tell my uncle? Would Paul and Silas report them to the officials in Rome?

They came to me hoping I would come to their defense as an ally. "The men are refusing to leave the jail," Marcellus exclaimed in disbelief. "They want us to go in person to release them! Would you go on our behalf and tell them the matter has been settled, and they don't need to press this any further?"

I hesitated a moment for effect before replying, "No. They apparently want to hear it directly from you. If you want to avoid any repercussions, I suggest you go to them."

Reluctantly, they went to the jail and apologized to Paul and Silas. In all my years, I have never seen a Roman official apologize for anything!

After they asked forgiveness and personally escorted Paul and Silas out of jail, the duumviri begged them to leave the city. They were afraid the mob would erupt again if Paul and Silas remained. Camillus and Marcellus knew if that occurred, they would be caught in the middle.

Paul assured them they would leave after attending to some matters in the city. Camillus and Marcellus nervously watched as Paul and Silas walked to my home. When they arrived, Paul told me, "The Spirit of the Lord has shown me my work here is done. You and your household, together with Aeropos and his household, are the ones the Spirit will use to make the Gospel known to the rest of the city. You will be His witnesses now!"

"But there is so much we have to learn," I said. "How can we learn if there is no one here to teach us?"

"The Spirit of God will guide you in all truth through the Torah you have and the witness about Jesus you have received," Paul replied. "Also, I have come to believe the Lord led Luke here to train up leaders in Philippi. He will remain and assist in that work until he has completed his task."

Paul sent word for Aeropos to come join us as he shared more words of encouragement. Then just before Silas, Timothy, and he left town, Paul said to us, *"Remain faithful to the things you have been taught. You know they are true, for you know you can trust those who taught you."*[(4)]

Later that day, after the men had departed, Rumena arrived at my home. "Matron, is the one they call Paul here?" she asked.

"No, he and his companions have left the city," I replied. "Why do you seek him?"

"Because he has set me free," Rumena answered. "For as long as I can remember, I have been enslaved by a spirit within me and masters who owned me. I have never been able to go where I wanted to go or do what I wanted to do. But ever since Paul told the spirit to come out of me, I have been set free. The spirit is no longer within me, and my masters have told me to leave them because I can no longer make them wealthy.

"At first, I was in despair, not knowing what I should do. I have always had someone to tell me what to do, but now I am free. I came to ask Paul's advice since he was the one who freed me."

"Rumena, Paul did not set you free. He may have been the one you heard speak the words, but the name of the One who set you free is Jesus. He is the Son of the living God, and He came to earth to set us all free from our sins. Twenty-two years ago, He was crucified on a cross as a sacrifice for our sins. But three days later He rose from the grave just as God promised He would do. He is not dead in a grave. He is alive!

"Think about it! We have always been told that we are to sacrifice ourselves for our gods, but He is a God who sacrificed Himself for us. He came so that you, and I, and Paul could be set free – as well as anyone else who repents of their sins and believes in Him. I was set free just a few days before Paul spoke those words to you.

"Yes, you have been set free," I continued. "But you still have one thing to do. If Paul were here, he would tell you to do the same thing he told me: 'repent of your sins, turn to God, and be baptized in the name of Jesus Christ.'"

"Then that is what I will do," Rumena said, smiling through her tears. "I repent and believe, and I want to be baptized!"

We all walked down to the riverbank that afternoon and Luke baptized Rumena. She became my sister in Christ that day and she moved into my home as one of the members of my household. Her masters couldn't possibly have been more mistaken about her – for she is now a treasure of immeasurable worth!

19

THE CHURCH GROWS

~

*J*n the weeks following Paul's departure, we continued to see more men and women declare their belief in Jesus and follow Him in baptism. One of the first to do so was Naomi. I rejoiced in the knowledge that my trusted business partner was now also my sister in Christ.

There were about fifty people, both men and women, gathered at the river-bank that Sabbath morning. Many had come out of curiosity; word had spread about Paul's arrest and release the week before. Others had heard about Rumena's transformation. They had encountered her many times when she offered to tell their fortune. Now she told them what Jesus had done for her.

We read aloud from the Torah the account of God's promise to Abraham:

The Lord took Abram outside and said to him, "Look up into the sky and count the stars if you can. That's how many descendants you will have!" And Abram believed the Lord, and the Lord counted him as righteous because of his faith.[1]

Then Luke told us, "Just as Abraham believed God, and God counted him as righteous because of his faith, the real children of Abraham are those who put their faith in God. What's more, the Scriptures looked forward to this time when God would make us Gentiles right in His sight because of our faith. God proclaimed this good news to Abraham long ago when He said, 'All nations will be blessed through you.' So all who put their faith in Christ share the same blessing Abraham received because of his faith."

In addition to Naomi, two other women – Euodia and Syntyche – and a man named Epaphroditus repented of their sins, placed their faith in Christ, and were baptized that day. All of us were excited to share our newfound faith with everyone we could. We began gathering each night in my home to read God's Word and learn more about Jesus. Our numbers continued to increase until we eventually had to move outside.

The large gathering began to draw the attention of my neighbors – the duumviri. Anytime large crowds gathered, the duumviri were always watchful to ensure the gathering was not fostering rebellion against Rome. I expected a visit from them soon – and I was not disappointed.

Camillus and Marcellus arrived at my home under the pretense of paying a social visit, but the conversation soon took a turn. "Lydia," Camillus began, "we have been watching the nightly gatherings outside your home with growing interest. We know some of the people are Jews, but many like yourself and our city jailer are not. As you know, we have been watching the Jews to make sure they do not disrupt our city with their beliefs. However, as we understand it, you are now hosting this gathering to worship and teach about the God of the Jews. Is that true?"

"Many of us who are gathered believe the God of the Jews is the one true God – the Creator of us all," I replied. "Like you, I have heard the many stories over the years about the Greek gods, the Roman gods, and the Macedonian gods. But I have always found those stories to be myths and fables with no basis in fact. But a few years ago, I was introduced to

Jehovah God – the God of the Jews. And there is too much historical and scientific fact to dispute His existence.

"But I didn't come to believe in Him until I learned He had sent His Son, Jesus, to suffer death on a Roman cross as the sacrifice for our sin. He died as a sacrifice for us all. But He didn't remain in the grave, He rose again. I know of no other god who was willing to lay down his life for me. I know of no other god who has died and come back from the dead. And yes, I worship Him . . . because He is worthy of my worship."

"We have heard about this Jesus," Marcellus responded. "We have been told that He declared Himself to be the King of the Jews and died a humiliating death on the cross. But He sounds as if He was a pathetic creature."

"He made the blind to see, the lame to walk, and the dead to come alive. He stilled the winds and the waves, cast out demons, and overcame death itself," I responded. "There isn't anything pathetic about Him, Marcellus!"

"The men you arrested – Paul and Silas – simply spoke in His name and a demon was cast out of Rumena. Just ask her former masters if they believe what happened to her was true. But then again, you don't need to, do you? They already told you it was true.

"So, what would you two have me do – deny the truth? Ignore the irrefutable reality I know to be true? My Roman education tells me to embrace truth. My grandfather Gaius taught me to stand for what is true! Would you now wish me to deny it because there are some who are close-minded to truth? No, I think not. I don't believe the men my uncle sponsored to be the duumviri of this city would show such little intellect and conviction.

"Rather, I invite you to no longer stand at a distance but come join our gathering tonight so you might better understand the truth. After all, as it is said, the truth will set you free!"

I truly hoped the duumviri would be open to seeking the truth of the Gospel, but they responded as I feared they would. "Thank you for your kind invitation, Lydia," Camillus replied, "but we will remain neutral on this matter. We will, however, guarantee you that no one will be permitted to disrupt your gathering. You, and your uncle, have our assurance of that."

The duumviri never questioned me again or threatened to disrupt our gathering. But sadly, they remained steadfast in their unbelief.

As the weeks passed, more men and women continued coming to faith. The Spirit of the Lord raised up those with spiritual gifts to be elders, deacons, and teachers. Among them were Aeropos, Epaphroditus, and Clement. I was grateful Paul had left Luke to shepherd us.

20

MY RETURN TO THYATIRA

~

*T*wo years later, I began to sense it was time for me to return to Thyatira. The church was growing in number and maturity under the pastoral leadership of Luke. Though we both knew he would one day soon move on, our elders believed God was raising up Clement to become the next pastor of the church. Luke was working closely with him to prepare him for the role. We all sensed God was raising up the needed leadership from within.

My business in Philippi was also prospering under the guiding hand of Naomi. I was confident the business would continue to thrive without my presence, despite Naomi's protests to the contrary. Also, she, Valeria, and I had all had a part in mentoring Rumena over the past two years and we were all equally confident in her ability to assist Naomi.

Valeria had recently turned nineteen, and I longed for her to spend some time in Rome with her grandfather Linus. But before she did, I wanted us to reunite with my mother in Thyatira. Janus had sent me word her health was declining, so I did not want to delay much longer.

The Spirit of the Lord was giving me confidence that my work here was done, so I arranged passage for Valeria, Sergius, Oppia, and me to return home. Before I departed, though, I knew there was one last thing I needed to do.

The duumviri were somewhat surprised to see me. Though we had by no means hidden from one another, our interactions had been limited over the past couple of years. But I knew my presence had been a deterrent against them doing anything that might harm the church.

"Camillus and Marcellus," I began, "I have come to thank you for all the assistance you have provided me since my arrival in Philippi. I plan to travel to Rome in the near future, and I will be certain to pass along my compliments to my uncle regarding you."

"You are most kind," Camillus replied humbly. "It has been our great privilege to assist you in whatever small way we have been able to do so. We do, however, regret you will be leaving our fair city." Then he added respectfully, "You have become one of our most prestigious residents, and we know your presence will be greatly missed by the entire city."

"Please be assured, Camillus, that I will continue to stay in close communication with my business associates here, no matter where I am. If I have any concerns, I will not hesitate to call upon you – or my uncle. And I am confident you will respond to my requests with the same level of courtesy you have always shown." The expressions on the two men's faces made it clear my point had not been lost on them. I could now leave knowing they would not create any problems for the church.

Three days later we boarded the ferry to Troas, and a week after that we arrived back in Thyatira. It was good to be home. Though God had done much in our lives through our time in Philippi, it had never felt like home. Valeria and I spent the next several days catching up on all the news with mother and Janus.

Janus had married while we were away. He and his wife, Clelia, now had a baby son. I was enjoying getting to know my little nephew, and Valeria, her little cousin. But Janus's reports about our mother had been understated. I wasn't prepared for how frail she had become. The strength and confidence she always exuded were gone.

Though I had written my family about my newfound faith in Jesus, I was grateful for this opportunity to tell them in person. I shared with them the truth I had learned from the Scriptures and the good news of Jesus. Valeria and I explained how Jesus had transformed our lives and the lives of so many in Philippi. I was grateful that mother, Janus, and Clelia all continued to ask me questions. They obviously had a desire to know and understand.

By our third day together, all three of them confessed their faith in Jesus. I baptized my brother in the river, and he and I together baptized our mother because of her frailty. Janus then baptized his wife. It was a great night of rejoicing as the rest of our household also placed their faith in Jesus and were baptized.

Two weeks later, I knew God had orchestrated the timing of our return to Thyatira. It was on that day we said goodbye to my mother as she passed from this life into the next. Because of her decision to follow Jesus, I knew I would see her again. We would be parted for a time, but we would spend all of eternity together in the presence of Jesus.

"Thank You, Lord," I prayed as I knelt beside her bed. "Thank You for allowing me to tell her about You and for granting me the opportunity to see her surrender her life to You. Thank You for saving her. And thank You for loving her – and all of us – so much that You sent Jesus."

To the best of our knowledge, there were no other believers in the city outside of our household, so there was no church. We made preparations to bury her body in a grave next to my father's. We knew our many friends would want to pay their respects. So we invited everyone to come to her graveside as Janus and I spoke.

As the oldest child, I did most of the speaking. It was the first time the Gospel was shared publicly in our city. Though I was grieving my mother's death, the Spirit of God gave me the strength and the words to share. I told them how I had placed my faith and trust in Jesus, as had my mother and the rest of our family. "We know right where our mother is. She's with Jesus! We will see her again . . . and so can you!"

21

RESISTANCE FROM THE GUILDS

~

*a*fter my mother's body had been committed to the ground, many friends returned home with us for a meal. I was overwhelmed by the number who told me they wanted to hear more about Jesus. After we ate, I invited those who wanted to learn more to stay.

Well into the evening I told them, "Since we were children, we have been told to seek the gods. Well, I am here to tell you about the *God who made the world and everything in it. Since He is Lord of heaven and earth, He doesn't live in man-made temples like Apollo, or the other gods of the Romans and the Greeks. Human hands can't serve His needs – for He has no needs. He himself gives life and breath to everything, and He satisfies every need.*

"From one man He created all the nations throughout the whole earth. He decided beforehand when they should rise and fall, and He determined their boundaries. His purpose was for the nations to seek after Him and perhaps feel their way toward Him and find Him – though He is not far from any one of us.

"For in Him we live and move and exist. As some of our own poets have said, 'We are His offspring.' And since this is true, we shouldn't think of God as an idol designed by craftsmen from gold or silver or stone.

"God overlooked people's ignorance about these things in earlier times, but now He commands everyone everywhere to repent of their sins and turn to Him. For He has set a day for judging the world with justice by the Man He has appointed, and He proved to everyone who this is by raising Him from the dead.[1]

"And that Man's name is Jesus. But He is not any man. He is God Himself who took on flesh as the Son of God and came to live among His creation. He lived and ate and breathed just as we do – with one important difference: He never sinned. Then when the time was right, Jehovah God permitted His Son to be crucified on a cross and His blood shed as the sacrifice for our sins.

"But though He was dead, three days later He rose from the grave. He lived, and died, and rose again so we might be redeemed from our sin. He paid the price, and all we must do to receive His redemption is to believe in Him, repent of our sins, and receive His forgiveness. As a man once told me, 'Repent, believe on His name, and be baptized!'"

Before the evening was over, twenty of our friends and neighbors had believed in Jesus and were baptized in the river! Every night afterward, those friends and others they brought gathered to hear more about Jesus. Each night a different person would share their testimony and the Gospel, and each night we saw more people believe and be baptized.

As I looked out over the growing crowd each evening I prayed, "Lord, to whom should we turn to shepherd these people? Luke is not here, neither is Paul, nor Silas, nor Timothy. What would You have us do?"

And I believe I heard the Spirit of the Lord reply, "I am not raising up followers of Paul, or Luke, or Silas, or Timothy. Neither am I raising up followers of Lydia or Janus. I am raising up followers of Jesus. Trust me to shepherd My people."

By faith, we took it a day at a time and saw God raise up teachers and leaders from within our midst. By His Spirit, He gave each one gifts according to the needs of the church – which He grew and nurtured.

But that growth was not without opposition. Every month the guild sponsored feasts for its members that involved worship of the emperor together with Apollo and other local pagan deities. The worship of those gods involved sexual immorality. Before I had become a follower of Jesus, those practices had not bothered me. But now Janus and I realized we could no longer continue to maintain our seats on the guild.

The guild did not take kindly to our position. Neither did they take kindly to what they saw as a threat against guild-led life in Thyatira. Not to participate in their pagan practices placed us at significant economic risk, some threatened, particularly if we wanted to continue to be successful in business and society.

But ours was the most successful dye and cloth business in Thyatira. We alone had a presence in Asia, Italy, and Macedonia. We were the recognized leaders of our trade – and by extension, the leaders of our guild – the same guild we were now rejecting. The other members knew they would be hard-pressed to compete against our business. We had the best dyes, the finest linens, and the most established and elite client base. We could survive without the guild – but the guild would suffer without us.

So, the guild leaders decided to attack us in the one place they felt we were vulnerable – the church. First, they pressured seekers or recent followers of Jesus by telling them it was fine for Janus and me to profess Jesus because we were successful and did not depend on the guild's support for our livelihood. But that was not the case for everyone else. The guild threatened to ruin them financially if they continued to pursue this Jesus.

Second, they began to stir up the rest of the city against the church saying, *"Brothers, you know that much of your wealth comes from the manufacture of shrines and goods used in the worship of the sun god Apollo. These followers of the One they call Jesus are attempting to persuade our citizens that Apollo is not a god at all. We're not just talking about the loss of respect for our businesses. We're also concerned that our magnificent god Apollo will be robbed of his prestige.*[2] We must convince our neighbors who have turned to this Jesus to put an end to their practice. Go to your neighbors who have been deceived and make them see the truth!"

$\sim$

22

RETURNING TO ROME

~

*D*espite those attempts by the guild and the persecution by their neighbors, the church remained strong and banded together. We all sold many of our possessions and shared the proceeds with those in need. As our neighbors witnessed how we cared for one another, the persecution died down. As a matter of fact, many of them came seeking to know more about Jesus.

Eventually the guild abandoned its pagan practices as more members became followers of Jesus. Many in our city still worshiped their false gods, but the church was growing, and the city was changing – for the better.

I began to sense the Spirit of the Lord telling me now was the time to take Valeria to Rome. I had no idea what the journey would bring, but I knew it would be a good opportunity for Valeria. Plus, I longed to see my uncle and his family, as well as Linus. Three weeks later, Valeria and I, together with Sergius and Oppia, set out for Rome.

After three weeks of travel, we found ourselves on the boat headed upriver toward Rome. I delighted in how Valeria reacted to the sights of the city as they came into view. I remembered my first view of the city nearly thirty years earlier. I understood the wonderment and amazement she was experiencing.

Even I was surprised by how much the city had changed during my twenty-four year absence. The Circus Maximus had been extended and was even more magnificent. More palatial homes were scattered throughout the city, and construction had just been completed on Emperor Nero's new grand palace. More of the streets had been paved with rocks, and everything appeared to be more pristine than I recalled.

I hoped my letter regarding our visit had reached Aurelius and Linus so they would be expecting us. When we arrived at Linus's home, he was eagerly awaiting us. Valeria was only three years old when he had last seen his granddaughter in Thyatira, and now she was a grown woman of twenty-two. We all had much to catch up on. I sent word to my Uncle Aurelius that we would call on him and his family the next day.

In the meantime, Valeria and I told Linus about our experiences in Philippi, which quickly turned to telling him how we had come to believe in Jesus. Linus listened intently, but he showed no interest in pursuing the subject further. We knew we needed to allow the Spirit of the Lord time to do His work in Linus, so we said nothing more.

Linus already knew about Naomi and the way she was leading our business in Philippi. He had become impressed with her ability through the messages we exchanged over the years. "And I have someone I want you to meet," Linus added. He sent word for someone in the house to join us.

When the man entered, Linus continued, "Lydia and Valeria, allow me to introduce my assistant, Eubulus. He has been assisting me for several years and in many ways has become like a son to me."

I could see from Valeria's reaction she was quite taken by this handsome young man who was a few years her senior – and he appeared to be equally taken with her. "Eubulus, it is a pleasure to meet you," I said. "We look forward to becoming better acquainted."

Our conversation continued well past dinner and into the evening. It was apparent that Valeria and Eubulus were not ready for the evening to end when I announced we needed to retire for the night. As I prepared for bed, I couldn't help but reflect on the many similarities between Eubulus and my Lucius.

The next day, we went to visit my Uncle Aurelius. He had aged greatly since I last saw him, particularly since the death of his wife, my Aunt Diana, one year earlier. He confided that he was considering stepping down from the senate and turning his seat over to his son, Pudens. As if on cue, my cousin and his wife, Priscilla, walked into the room to join us. I was happy to see that Pudens and his wife were quite capable of assuming the roles of master and mistress of this home.

During our time together, Valeria and I both shared about our decision to place our faith in Jesus. I was pleased and surprised when Pudens spoke up. "Well, if you are followers of Jesus of Nazareth then I must introduce you to my friend, Pontius Aquila. He was in Jerusalem when Jesus was crucified. In fact, his father was the prefect who condemned Him to death."

I could not believe my ears. Though Paul had told me he had seen Jesus in different ways over the years, I had yet to meet anyone who had actually seen Him in Jerusalem. "I look forward to meeting him," I replied.

"Then we will arrange for him and his mother to join us for dinner very soon," Pudens replied, sensing my excitement.

Two weeks later, Valeria and I were invited to join my uncle and cousin for dinner with Pontius Aquila and his mother, Claudia. As the night progressed, I asked them to tell us everything they knew of Jesus.

"I spent my youth in the palace in Caesarea Maritima," Pontius Aquila began. "My mother and I were both in Jerusalem when the religious leaders brought Jesus of Nazareth before my father, Pontius Pilate. I watched from the roof as my father condemned Jesus to die on the cross. My father knew He was innocent, and so did my mother and I.

"Tears flowed down our cheeks as we watched my father come before that crowd and refuse to stand up for what he knew was right. I watched in shame as he ceremoniously washed his hands. It was a turning point in my life. Until that moment, I would have followed my father anywhere.

"When the soldiers led Jesus to the cross, I covered myself with a cloak and followed from a distance. I watched as He was crucified under my father's order. I knew He was not only an innocent man, falsely accused – I knew He was a righteous man and so did my mother. I later heard He had risen from the grave, though my father denied the reports. He contended that Jesus's disciples had moved His body. But I never believed that.

"Lydia, Pudens tells me you are a follower of Jesus. Please tell us how that came to be."

~

23

ARRESTED!

～

*I*t was about a week later Valeria and I joined my uncle for dinner at his home again. I was delighted to find Pudens and Priscilla were also there, as well as Pontius Aquila. All three were animatedly discussing something that had occurred earlier that day.

"Cousin Lydia," Pudens greeted me, "we have the most exciting news to share with you! Today, Priscilla and I became followers of Jesus! We repented of our sins, placed our faith in Him, and were baptized!"

I was overjoyed. "How did you come to your decision?" I asked. "I know you have been considering all we have spoken about these past few weeks. But how did the Spirit of the Lord lead you to make that decision today?"

"We were talking with Aquila, and he told us he and his mother had just been baptized two days ago," Pudens answered. "As he spoke, Priscilla and I looked at each other and asked, 'What is keeping us from being baptized?' We knew at that moment we believed, and if we delayed any longer we would be disobeying what God was telling us to do. So earlier today we went to the river and Aquila's new friend, Luke, baptized us."

I wondered if it could be the same Luke I knew. "Who is this Luke and how do you know him, Aquila?"

"He is a friend of the apostle Paul who led my mother and me to faith in Jesus three nights ago," Aquila answered. "He told us the same good news you had shared with us a few weeks ago, and as he did, we knew we believed. The truth is, we believed in Jerusalem all those years ago; we just failed to act on what we believed."

"Where did you see Paul?" I asked excitedly. "Is he here in Rome? And Luke is with him?"

I went on to tell them how it had been Paul who preached the Gospel to Valeria and me and baptized us in Philippi. "Then Luke stayed in my home for two years until I returned to Thyatira," I explained. "Where are these men? Can we go get them and have them come join us for dinner?"

I could not contain my excitement over this news. My cousins were now my brother and sister in Christ, and my dear friends, Paul and Luke, were here in the city!

"Paul can't come join us, Lydia," Aquila replied slowly. "He is under house arrest, awaiting a hearing before Caesar."

"He's what?" I asked in disbelief. "How is it he was arrested and how is it he is here? Can I see him? Will you take me to him?"

"Yes, you can see him. I will take you tomorrow," Aquila answered. "I will let him explain why he is here. But I will tell you he is here because God led him here. His three-year journey to get here is a testimony of God's ability to order our steps to accomplish His purpose – no matter how unlikely it may appear. And because of God's faithfulness, Priscilla, Pudens, and I stand before you tonight as trophies of God's grace – just like you and Valeria.

Suddenly Uncle Aurelius spoke up. He had obviously been listening to our conversation. "I, too, have now repented and believed. What must I do to be baptized?"

Little had I known when I set out to come for dinner that the evening would become such a great night of celebration! Every living member of my family had now come to faith in Jesus!

The next day, Aquila and Pudens took me to visit Paul. I discovered he was staying in rooms directly below those of Eubulus. Ironically, the house he was staying in was owned by Eubulus's family. Apparently, everyone in my circle of influence knew Paul was in Rome except me! And what's more, Eubulus had just placed his faith in Jesus that morning!

Paul explained how he had been falsely accused and arrested by the religious leaders in Jerusalem. I was aware of Paul's history of being falsely accused and wrongfully imprisoned, but I was amazed as I listened to his account of the two long years he had awaited trial in Caesarea Maritima, his appeal to Caesar, and his treacherous voyage to Rome.[1]

As I told him about the church the Spirit had birthed in Thyatira, it was his turn to rejoice. He said he was sending letters of encouragement to the churches in Asia and Macedonia, and he would also send one to Thyatira. It was obvious Paul's eyesight was continuing to fail, so I asked how he was writing those letters. He quickly introduced me to Aristarchus, his companion and secretary.

Paul remained chained between two soldiers the entire time we spoke. But I knew they were brothers in Christ by their reactions to what was being said. I joined Paul in prayer that God would soon open the door for him to share the Gospel with Emperor Nero. With what I had witnessed over the past twenty-four hours, I was certain a mighty movement of God was about to take place across Rome!

And God was not done working in my family. Aquila and Eubulus accompanied me back to Linus's home for the night. As we told him about our day, he too surrendered his life to Jesus. Arrangements were made for Eubulus and him to be baptized the next morning.

Everyone I partnered with in business was now also a brother or sister in Christ. Regardless of whether our business continued to be a financial success, I was jubilant to realize we were now all united in Christ's purpose and mission!

∾

24

NEWS FROM PHILIPPI

~

 few months later, Valeria and I were pleased when Epaphroditus arrived in Rome to see Paul. He stayed with Paul in his rooms, together with Luke and Aristarchus, so they could all serve Paul and assist him with errands. Frequently during our visits with Paul, we would catch up on news about the church in Philippi. Though I received periodic reports from Naomi, it was entirely different to hear Epaphroditus's detailed accounts firsthand of how God was growing the church – numerically and in maturity.

"Clement is continuing to serve as pastor of the church," he told us. Luke had informed me about the ease of transition when he left Philippi five years earlier to rejoin Paul.

"Clement has grown in knowledge and maturity," Epaphroditus continued, "and has been, without any doubt, the man God chose and equipped to pastor the church. Under his leadership, the saints continue to grow in knowledge and understanding of the Word.

"The carpenter, Syzygus, has become an elder in the church. You may recall he came to faith while Paul was still with us and has become a steadfast witness who is undeniably filled with the Holy Spirit. The church relies on him greatly for his godly wisdom."

Other good news was that Aeropos had been elevated from his role as jailer to one of the magistrates of the city, assisting the duumviri. That happened as a result of the night Paul and Silas had been entrusted to his care. When word reached the duumviri that all the prison doors had opened that night and all the chains had fallen off every prisoner, Aeropos was recognized for his valiant effort in keeping every prisoner from escaping.

"Aeropos knew it was solely the work of the Spirit of the Lord," Epaphroditus recounted, "and he tried to communicate that to the duumviri. But they had ignored what they considered his humility and promoted him for his bravery and quick thinking. Though we all knew they were failing to acknowledge who was truly responsible, we also knew God was using it to place one of His servants in a position of authority for the furtherance of His purpose."

Epaphroditus went on to say that because of Aeropos's new position, he had unlimited access to the duumviri – which gave him opportunities to tell Camillus what had truly taken place. Though my own access to the duumviri had been limited by Marcellus during my last two years in the city, apparently the Spirit of God had silently been at work in the heart of Camillus.

On multiple occasions, when just the two of them were together, Camillus had questioned Aeropos about that night. Aeropos had the opportunity to share the Gospel with him, and one evening Camillus surrendered his life to Jesus. When I heard the news, I was thrilled and began to praise the Lord for His saving work!

"Over the years," Epaphroditus added, "Camillus has grown bold in his witness and has become one of the leaders in the church. Marcellus has yet to become a follower of Jesus, but the church has been able to prosper in a season of newfound freedoms without any concern of reprisal from the magistrates."

When the church heard about Paul's arrest and imprisonment, they immediately dispatched Epaphroditus as one of the elders to Rome. Since the officials in Caesarea Maritima would have released Paul if he had not appealed to Caesar, he was burdened with the cost for his own transportation to Rome, the salaries of those who accompanied him, the cost of his housing, and the wages of the guards who were chained to him.

The Philippian church took up an offering to assist Paul with those living expenses, just as many of us did. Epaphroditus brought the church's offering along with a cloak Rumena had sewn for him.

I was distressed to hear my good friends Euodia and Syntyche were at odds with each other. Apparently, their fighting was dividing the church and placing the unity of the body in jeopardy. Paul was troubled by this news, as well.

"I will need to send you back to Philippi with instructions for Syzygus to help them settle their dispute," Paul told Epaphroditus. "Since he is an elder, and their senior by a few years, he is in the best position to give them counsel. I'm afraid they may not listen to Clement because of his young age."

Several days later, Epaphroditus fell ill with fever. We feared he had contracted the illness from Uncle Aurelius, who was now also confined to his bed. We knew Epaphroditus could no longer stay with Paul for fear he and the others might contract it. Pudens suggested Epaphroditus stay at his father's home so the same physicians could attend to them both.

The two men's conditions deteriorated and became critical. Neither was showing any sign of improvement despite the care of the city's finest physicians. Luke, at great personal risk, quarantined himself in my uncle's home so he could provide additional care for them.

Despite those best efforts, my uncle died. Though Pudens, Priscilla, Valeria, and I grieved his death, we had peace knowing he and my mother had now been reunited, and we would all see him again. Because of his position in the senate, there typically would have been an elaborate funeral proceeding. Instead, due to a growing fear across the city about the contagion of the fever, we quietly buried him.

We were afraid Epaphroditus would soon follow my uncle in death. But, in God's mercy, he miraculously recovered. And by God's grace, none of the rest of us contracted the fever. It reminded us that God knows – and controls – the number of our days. He obviously had more for all of us to accomplish for His glory. Because as Paul often said, *"He who began a good work in you will complete it!"*[1]

25

MY RETURN TO PHILIPPI

〜

*H*aving received reports about many of the churches, Paul proceeded to write each of them a letter. One of those letters was addressed to the church in Philippi, and Paul wanted Epaphroditus to deliver it. Several of us felt he had not yet recovered enough to make the journey by himself.

As we discussed it, I sensed the Spirit leading Sergius, Oppia, and me to make the journey with him. Valeria, on the other hand, told me she wanted to remain in Rome. I knew her grandfather and her older cousin Pudens, who had now taken his father's seat in the senate, would keep a watchful eye on her. Valeria had begun to find her place in Roman society, and she was becoming one of the leaders of the new church here.

My heart ached to be separated from her, but I knew it was time. She was a twenty-seven-year-old woman, and a relationship was budding between her and Eubulus. When I looked at her, I saw myself: an independent young woman with plans to change the world – for the sake of the King- dom. It was time for me to grant her that independence.

She and Eubulus accompanied us to the docks where Epaphroditus, Sergius, Oppia, and I boarded a Macedonian merchant ship. It was a three-week journey with stops along the way in Messana, Athens, Miletus, and Troas. When we landed in Miletus, I realized I was only a short distance over land from Thyatira, but that was not my destination.

When we finally arrived in Philippi, the church – made up of old friends and new – greeted us warmly. I had been away for eight years, but in some ways, it was if I never left as we picked right back up on conversations. The church had grown to the point the body was now gathering in multiple locations around the city.

None greeted us more warmly than Camillus. He was without question a changed man, and I rejoiced with him in the work God had done in his life. When we told him we were delivering a letter from Paul to the church, Camillus said he would arrange for us to use the city's amphitheater that night so everyone could meet together to hear what Paul had written.

When it was time for Epaphroditus to address the gathering, he began by saying, "The church in Philippi is probably closer to Paul's heart than any other. Our love for him and his for us has been deeply rooted from the start. He writes to thank us for our constant help throughout his times of need, but he also wants to encourage us to remain true to the Lord."

He then began to read Paul's letter:

"I am writing to all of God's holy people in Philippi who belong to Christ Jesus, including the church leaders and deacons. May God our Father and the Lord Jesus Christ give you grace and peace.

"Every time I think of you, I give thanks to my God. Whenever I pray, I make my requests for all of you with joy, for you have been my partners in spreading the Good News about Christ from the time you first heard it until now. And I am certain that God, who began the good work within you, will continue His work until it is finally finished on the day when Christ Jesus returns." [1]

He continued reading the letter of exhortation and then came to this specific message:

"Therefore, my dear brothers and sisters, stay true to the Lord. I love you and long to see you, dear friends, for you are my joy and the crown I receive for my work.

"Now I appeal to Euodia and Syntyche. Please, because you belong to the Lord, settle your disagreement. And I ask you, loyal Syzygus, to help these two women, for they worked hard with me in telling others the Good News. They worked along with Clement and the rest of my co-workers, whose names are written in the Book of Life."[2]

I looked over at Euodia and Syntyche, whom I loved as sisters. These two women and I had been together at that very first prayer gathering at the riverbank. They had been closer than sisters. But now they were estranged, and it was affecting the church. The two women looked embarrassed as Epaphroditus read Paul's words. But more than that, their expressions registered a deep sense of remorse. I prayed that the Spirit would bring reconciliation and restoration to my friends – and I was confident He would.

Epaphroditus continued:

"Fix your thoughts on what is true and honorable and right. Think about things that are pure and lovely and admirable. Think about things that are excellent and worthy of praise. Keep putting into practice all you learned from me and heard from me and saw me doing, and the God of peace will be with you."[3]

When Epaphroditus finished, the church members embraced one another, cried with each other, and praised the Lord together for His goodness. Yes, the One who had begun the work would complete it, and they were ready to follow Him to that end – even Euodia and Syntyche.

Several months later, I learned that Paul had been released from his house arrest in Rome. His accusers from Jerusalem never made an appearance in Rome, so he could make no appeal if there was no one to make a charge. Accordingly, Pontius Aquila and Pudens appealed for his release, and it was granted. He hadn't been given the opportunity to proclaim the Good News to Emperor Nero, but the Spirit had given him the opportunity to preach to many others.

Paul traveled for five years after that, including a three-month stay in Philippi. During that time, we received news that Emperor Nero had ordered the apostle Peter be crucified on a cross in Rome. The winds of persecution were beginning to blow throughout the empire, fanned by the flames in Rome. These had become uncertain times, but we clung to the certainty of our Savior.

By the time Paul arrived in Philippi, I had already returned to Thyatira. He sent me a message that he would soon come and spend time with the church there. But he only made it as far as Troas. I soon received another message that Paul had again been arrested and was being taken to Rome – not to appeal to the emperor but to be executed by him.

I feared for Paul . . . but with all of the unrest in the city, I also feared for Valeria. I immediately set out for Rome.

26

A CITY IN FLAMES

~

*T*his time as Sergius, Oppia, and I traveled to Rome from the new harbor of Portus, the city looked very different. It had been over two-and-one-half years since the fire had destroyed a good deal of the city. Though much rebuilding had already occurred, there still were many physical reminders of the devastation that had taken place.

But much more visible was the deathly pallor that had now befallen the city. Even from the river, I could see crosses scattered along the horizon, casting their shadows of death in every corner of the city. I wept as I saw my brothers and sisters hanging on crosses. I asked the Lord to comfort them and give them strength to endure their final moments of agony before they entered His presence.

The sight made me even more afraid for Valeria and my family and friends who were followers of Jesus. When we arrived in the city, we immediately made our way to Valeria's home. She and Eubulus had now been married for five years and she had recently given birth to my granddaughter, Olivia. My heart slowed to a normal rhythm as soon as I saw Valeria and her infant daughter. It was a moment of overwhelming joy in the midst of the oppressive horror that surrounded us.

After Valeria placed my granddaughter in my arms, she began to update me on all that was happening. "All our family members are safe and have not received any threats. Most of our brothers and sisters in Christ who are being crucified have been brought to Rome from other places, just like Paul. Emperor Nero apparently does not want to risk inciting a revolt of Roman citizens."

"How did this all start?" I asked.

"The fire in the city broke out in one of the cook shops situated near the Circus Maximus," Valeria replied. "It was a windy day, and the fire spread quickly. It took nine days before it could be contained. As you have already seen, the fire destroyed a substantial part of the city, leaving many dead and many others homeless. It was only by God's grace that our home was spared, as well as the homes of Grandfather Linus and cousin Pudens.

"The surviving citizens of Rome became incensed against Emperor Nero. Many were shouting in the streets, 'Why did the emperor not lead the city to react more quickly to extinguish the fire?' There were some who accused him of setting the fire himself.

"He quickly took action to divert the blame from himself to the Christians. He announced we were a threat to the empire. He accused us of being troublemakers who followed a leader who had been crucified in Jerusalem because of His acts of rebellion. He told the entire empire they needed to be purged of Christians or risk being destroyed. He sent out troops to arrest believers. Our Christian brothers in the senate, like Pudens and Aquila, together with officers of the military, attempted to reason with him – but he would not listen.

"He began gathering up Christians from around the empire and having them crucified on the streets of Rome. He learned that the apostle Peter was one of the leaders of the movement and was here in Rome. He sent out soldiers to apprehend him at once. There was no trial; Nero had him crucified immediately.

"We only recently learned Paul was here. He was held in the dungeon for several weeks before we received the news when Luke and Aristarchus arrived. As soon as we heard, Pudens and Aquila began making pleas on his behalf with fellow members of the senate. But their influence has greatly diminished because they are Christians. Though their efforts were unsuccessful, they were able to arrange for Luke and Aristarchus to stay with Paul in his cell so he would not be alone.

"One of our Christian brothers is an officer in the Praetorian guard, and he is able to deliver food and clothing to Paul and the others on occasion. He has become our only lifeline of communication with Paul. Short of miraculous intervention by God, Paul will soon be executed. Apparently, the only detail in question is the form of execution to be used.

"Paul has declared he is unworthy to be executed in the same way as our Lord. He pled before the judge that since he is a Roman citizen that he be beheaded according to the law. There has been a delay in his execution awaiting that decision. Apparently, Emperor Nero has been called upon to decide his fate. Word could come at any moment.

"The church is gathering in secret small groups each night to pray for Paul and all of those who are being apprehended and sentenced to death. Tonight, we will gather in grandfather's home, and you will join us."

When Eubulus, Valeria, Olivia, my servants, and I arrived, I was again overcome with conflicting emotions. I wanted to spend some time with Linus before the others arrived. Though he was now eighty-two years of age, he had continued to remain remarkably active. Eubulus was now attending to most of the details of our business, but Linus still maintained a visible presence. He also had been actively serving as an elder of the Roman church almost since its inception.

I fondly remembered the first time I had met him at my grandparents' home almost forty-two years earlier. I thought back to those carefree days. With the passing of so many loved ones in my life, Linus had been my one constant over the years. But as I looked at him that night, I realized the events surrounding us were taking a heavy toll on him. I knew one day soon he would be passing on to his reward in heaven.

Pudens and Priscilla, Aquila and his mother, Claudia, who was also looking frail, and a few others I did not know assembled at Linus's home and we began to pray.

We continued to meet together nightly for prayer for several months – until the night Luke and Aristarchus joined us. Paul had been beheaded that day. He had entered into the eternal presence of his Lord. He had finished his race.

Luke showed us Paul's last words, written in his own hand:

> "HERE IS MY FINAL GREETING IN MY OWN HAND – PAUL.
> REMEMBER MY CHAINS.
> MAY THE GRACE OF GOD BE WITH YOU." [1]

~

27

FINISHING MY RACE

~

I decided I would stay in Rome. I was approaching sixty years of age, and I wanted to live out the rest of my life close to my daughter and granddaughter. I wanted to be an encouragement and support to them, just like my mother had been to me.

The political landscape soon changed dramatically when Emperor Nero was declared a public enemy by the senate, largely due to the efforts of Pudens and Aquila. Within a few months of Paul's death, Nero committed suicide, resulting in an end to the persecution of Christians. We praised God for His mercy and deliverance.

But Rome continued in political turmoil. During the eighteen months following Nero's death, we were ruled by four different emperors, the fourth of which – Emperor Vespasian – assumed his rule by executing his predecessor through a military takeover. The city remained under a cloud of oppression. Though Christians were no longer being persecuted, no one outside the church knew whom they could trust. The group in power today could be tomorrow's enemy. Everyday interactions between people on the streets became cautious and stilted; relationships became strained.

As a result of the tensions, our trade in the city was impacted. Gratefully, many of our patrons had been working with us for a long time, so we weren't as affected as other businesses. In the midst of that time, Linus passed away peacefully in his sleep. The physicians told us his heart had simply stopped beating. I was grateful he had not suffered.

Most of our community came together to remember his life and the impact he had on so many. He finished his race well, and I rejoiced in the knowledge of how many lives he touched as each one took a moment to tell me. Though he would have been the first to tell you he wasn't a preacher or a teacher like Paul, many had come to believe in Jesus because of the testimony of his life. I would miss him – but I knew it would only be for a season.

As I looked ahead at what was in store for our business, I was thankful the partnership he and my father had forged so many years earlier remained strong. They had laid a solid foundation on which I was able to build. And by all indications, it would continue to prosper. Valeria was assuming more of my role as Eubulus managed our trade in Rome, Naomi continued to do so in Philippi, and Janus was grooming his son to manage the work in Thyatira. And I knew each one would add his or her unique stamp to it as well. It was a business God had prospered for His Kingdom purpose as we sought to further His mission and honor Him through all our dealings.

One year after Linus died, Emperor Vespasian dispatched his army to besiege the city of Jerusalem. During the previous four years, Jewish leaders had led their people in anti-tax protests and attacks on Roman citizens who were in positions of authority. The attacks had now escalated into full-scale rebellion. After only a few short months, Jerusalem fell, and the Temple was destroyed.

The church in Rome gathered to pray for our brothers and sisters in Jerusalem. We knew the seeds of the Gospel had first been planted there forty years earlier through the crucifixion and resurrection of our Lord. The church had soon scattered, and in so doing the Gospel had been spread throughout Asia, Macedonia, and Europe by Paul and others. We were the product of their faithfulness. We were fruit the Spirit of the Lord had produced from their vineyard.

Several months later, we received word the church had again scattered from Jerusalem as a result of the siege. The apostle John – the only original apostle still living in Jerusalem at the time – traveled to Asia, stopping to spend time with each of the churches along the way, including Thyatira. Janus wrote me of how God had used John to encourage the Thyatiran church. Even though Paul never made it to Thyatira, God had another plan – and that plan included John. Along the way, John also stopped at Laodicea, Philadelphia, Sardis, Pergamum, and Smyrna before settling in Ephesus to pastor the church there.

It caused me to remember something I had heard Paul say on multiple occasions:

"I planted the seed in your hearts, and another watered it, but it was God who made it grow. It's not important who does the planting, or who does the watering. What's important is that God makes the seed grow. The one who plants and the one who waters work together with the same purpose. And both will be rewarded for their own hard work. For we are both God's workers. And you are God's field. You are God's building."[1]

Another twenty years has now passed. My granddaughter Olivia is preparing to marry a godly young man who has been assisting Valeria and Eubulus in the business here in Rome. God has greatly blessed our business and our family. I have so much for which I am thankful.

As the end of my life on this earth approaches, I am blessed that God has permitted me to be part of three churches – in Philippi, Thyatira, and Rome. I have seen the principle of sowing, planting, and harvesting lived out in each one of those churches. And I've seen that the life cycle continues. I have seen the church when it pursues Jesus wholeheartedly, when it becomes distracted by worldly desires, and when it is led away from truth by an instrument of Satan.

I understand from Janus there is one now who has planted herself within the body of Thyatira and is sowing seeds of destruction and division. The task of correction will now fall to someone else. I trust the Lord to redeem her or cast her out. I trust Him to protect His church and bring to perfection that which He has begun.

As Paul wrote:

"I am certain that God, who began the good work within you, will continue His work until it is finally finished on the day when Christ Jesus returns."[2]

Until that day, may the grace of our Lord Jesus Christ be with you.

PLEASE HELP ME BY LEAVING A REVIEW!

i would be very grateful if you would leave a review of this book. Your feedback will be helpful to me in my future writing endeavors and will also assist others as they consider picking up a copy of the book.

To leave a review:

Go to: amazon.com/dp/1956866051

Or scan this QR code using your camera on your smartphone:

Thanks for your help!

∾

YOU WILL WANT TO READ ALL OF THE BOOKS IN "THE CALLED" SERIES

Stories of these ordinary men and women called by God to be used in extraordinary ways.

A Carpenter Called Joseph (Book 1)

A Prophet Called Isaiah (Book 2)

A Teacher Called Nicodemus (Book 3)

A Judge Called Deborah (Book 4)

A Merchant Called Lydia (Book 5)

A Friend Called Enoch (Book 6)

A Fisherman Called Simon (Book 7)

A Heroine Called Rahab (Book 8)

A Witness Called Mary (Book 9) releasing March 24

A Cupbearer Called Nehemiah (Book 10) releasing June 16

AVAILABLE IN PAPERBACK, LARGE PRINT, AND FOR KINDLE ON AMAZON.

Scan this QR code using your camera on your smartphone to see the entire series.

IF YOU ENJOYED THIS STORY ABOUT LYDIA ...

… you will want to read this novel about the life and journeys of the apostle Paul

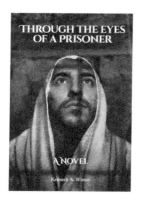

Paul was an unlikely candidate to become the apostle to the Gentiles … until the day he unexpectedly encountered Jesus. You are probably familiar with that part of his story, and perhaps much of what transpired in his life after that. **But two-thirds of his life story is not recorded in detail, though Paul gives us some hints in his letters.**

Through this fictional novel, we'll explore how God may have used those unrecorded portions of his life to prepare him for the mission that was being set before him. We'll follow him from his early years in Tarsus through his final days in Rome.

Throughout those years, Paul spent more time in a prison cell than we are ever told. It was a place where God continued to work in and through him. The mission never stopped because he was in prison; it simply took on a different form. Allow yourself to be challenged as you experience **a story of God's mission – through the eyes of a prisoner who ran the race that was put before him – and the faithfulness of God through it all.**

AVAILABLE IN PAPERBACK, LARGE PRINT, HARDCOVER, AND FOR KINDLE ON AMAZON.

To order your copy:

Go to: amazon.com/dp/1734934581

Or scan this QR code using your camera on your smartphone:

THROUGH THE EYES

... the complete *"THROUGH THE EYES"* SERIES

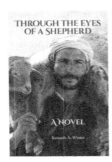  

Experience the truths of Scripture as these stories unfold through the lives and eyes of a shepherd, a spy and a prisoner. Rooted in biblical truth, these fictional novels will enable you to draw beside the storytellers as they worship the Baby in the manger, the Son who took up the cross, the Savior who conquered the grave, the Deliverer who parted the sea and the Eternal God who has always had a mission.

Through the Eyes of a Shepherd (Book 1)

Through the Eyes of a Spy (Book 2)

Through the Eyes of a Prisoner (Book 3)

AVAILABLE IN PAPERBACK, LARGE PRINT, AND FOR KINDLE ON AMAZON.

Scan this QR code using your camera on your smartphone to see the entire series on Amazon:

THE EYEWITNESSES COLLECTION

... you will also want to read "The Eyewitnesses" Collection

The first four books in these collections of short stories chronicle the first person eyewitness accounts of eighty-five men, women and children and their unique relationships with Jesus.

Little Did We Know – the advent of Jesus (Book 1)

Not Too Little To Know – the advent – ages 8 thru adult (Book 2)

The One Who Stood Before Us – the ministry and passion of Jesus (Book 3)

The Little Ones Who Came – the ministry and passion – ages 8 thru adult (Book 4)

The Patriarchs — eyewitnesses from the beginning — Adam through Moses tell their stories (Book 5) — releasing in 2023

AVAILABLE IN PAPERBACK, LARGE PRINT, AND FOR KINDLE ON AMAZON.

Scan this QR code using your camera on your smartphone to see the entire collection on Amazon:

LESSONS LEARNED IN THE WILDERNESS

The Lessons Learned In The Wilderness series

A non-fiction series of devotional studies

There are lessons that can only be learned in the wilderness experiences of our lives. As we see throughout the Bible, God is right there leading us each and every step of the way, if we will follow Him. Wherever we are, whatever we are experiencing, He will use it to enable us to experience His Person, witness His power and join Him in His mission.

The Journey Begins (Exodus) – Book 1

The Wandering Years (Numbers and Deuteronomy) – Book 2

Possessing The Promise (Joshua and Judges) – Book 3

Walking With The Master (The Gospels leading up to Palm Sunday) – Book 4

Taking Up The Cross (The Gospels – the passion through ascension) – Book 5

Until He Returns (The Book of Acts) – Book 6

The complete series is also available in two e-book boxsets or two single soft-cover print volumes.

AVAILABLE IN PAPERBACK AND FOR KINDLE ON AMAZON.

Scan this QR code using your camera on your smartphone to see the entire series on Amazon:

For more information, go to:

wildernesslessons.com or kenwinter.org

ALSO AVAILABLE AS AN AUDIOBOOK

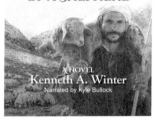

SCRIPTURE BIBLIOGRAPHY

~

Much of the story line of this book is taken from the Acts of the Apostles, the Epistle of Paul the Apostle to the Philippians, and The Revelation of Jesus Christ as recorded in Scripture. Certain fictional events or depictions of those events have been added.

Some of the dialogue in this story are direct quotations from Scripture. Here are the specific references for those quotations:

Chapter 14

[1] Isaiah 61:1-3

[2] Psalm 34:4-7

[3] Psalm 34:8

Chapter 15

[1] Acts 2:38

Chapter 16

(1) Acts 16:15

(2) Acts 16:9

(3) Acts 16:17

(4) Acts 16:18

Chapter 17

(1) Acts 16:20-21

(2) Acts 16:28

(3) Acts 16:30

Chapter 18

(1) Acts 16:35

(2) Acts 16:36

(3) Acts 16:37

(4) 2 Timothy 3:14

Chapter 19

(1) Genesis 15:5-6

Chapter 21

(1) Adapted from Acts 17:24-31

(2) Adapted from Acts 19:25-27

Chapter 23

(1) For the complete account of Paul's journey read Acts chapters 21 through 28

Chapter 24

(1) Philippians 1:6 (NKJ)

Chapter 25

(1) Philippians 1:1-6

(2) Philippians 4:1-3

(3) Philippians 4:8-9

Chapter 26

(1) Colossians 4:18

Chapter 27

(1) 1 Corinthians 3:6-9

(2) Philippians 1:6

Unless otherwise indicated, all Scripture quotations are taken from the *Holy Bible,* New Living Translation, copyright © 1996. Used by permission of Tyndale House Publishers, Inc., Wheaton, Illinois 60189. All rights reserved.

Scripture quotations marked (NKJ) are taken from the *New King James Version,* copyright © 1979, 1980, 1982 by Thomas Nelson, Inc., Nashville, Tennessee 37214. Used by permission.

LISTING OF CHARACTERS (ALPHABETICAL ORDER)

~

Many of the characters in this book are real people pulled directly from the pages of Scripture. i have not changed any details about a number of those individuals, except the addition of their interactions with fictional characters. They are noted below as "UN" (unchanged).

In other instances, fictional details have been added to real people to provide backgrounds about their lives where Scripture is silent. The intent is that you understand these were real people, whose lives were full of all of the many details that fill our own lives. They are noted as "FB" (fictional background).

In some instances, we are not told the names of certain individuals in the Bible. In those instances, where i have given them a name, as well as a fictional background, they are noted as "FN" (fictional name).

Lastly, some of the characters are purely fictional, added to convey the fictional elements of these stories. They are noted as "FC" (fictional character).

~

Aeropos – jailer in Philippi (FN)

Aristarchus – early believer in Thessalonica with noble background, companion of Paul (FB)

Aurelius – son of Gaius, husband of Diana, father of Pudens, member of senate (FC)

Caecilia – daughter of Gaius, wife of Evander, mother of Lydia & Janus (FC)

Camillus – one of the duumviri of Philippi (FN)

Claudia – wife of Pontius Pilate, mother of Pontius Aquila II, friend of Paul (FB)

Clelia – wife of Janus, mother of unnamed son (FC)

Clement – pastor of Philippian church (FB)

Cornelia – wife of Gaius, mother of Aurelius & Caecilia, grandmother of Lydia (FC)

Diana – wife of Aurelius, mother of Pudens (FC)

Emperor Augustus – 1st Roman emperor (UN)

Emperor Caligula – 3rd Roman emperor (UN)

Emperor Claudius – 4th Roman emperor (UN)

Emperor Galba – 6th Roman emperor (UN)

Emperor Nero – 5th Roman emperor (UN)

Emperor Otho – 7th Roman emperor (UN)

Emperor Tiberius – 2nd Roman emperor (UN)

Emperor Vespasian – 9th Roman emperor (UN)

Emperor Vitellius – 8th Roman emperor (UN)

Empress Livia – wife of Emperor Augustus (UN)

Epaphroditus – leader in Philippian church, friend of Paul (FB)

Eubulus – associate of Linus, husband of Valeria, father of Olivia, friend of Paul (FB)

Euodia – part of prayer group at riverbank, leader of Philippian church (FB)

Evander – husband of Caecilia, father of Lydia & Janus, merchant of purple cloth (FC)

Gaius – husband of Cornelia, father of Aurelius & Caecilia, grandfather of Lydia, member of senate (FC)

Janus – son of Evander & Caecilia, brother of Lydia, husband of Clelia, father of unnamed son, merchant of purple cloth (FC)

John – apostle of Jesus, elder of Jerusalem church, pastor of Ephesian church (UN)

Linus – father of Lucius, father-in-law of Lydia, grandfather of Valeria, elder of church in Rome, merchant of purple cloth (FB)

Lucius – son of Linus, husband of Lydia, father of Valeria (FC)

Luke – physician, travel companion of Paul, pastor of Philippian church, writer of *The Gospel according to Luke* and *The Acts of the Apostles* (FB)

Lydia – daughter of Evander & Caecilia, wife of Lucius, mother of Valeria, grandmother of Olivia, merchant of purple cloth (FB)

Marcellus – one of the duumviri of Philippi (FN)

Marijana – mother of Evander, grandmother of Lydia & Janus (FC)

Naomi – Jewish business partner of Lydia in Philippi (FC)

Olivia – daughter of Eubulus & Valeria, granddaughter of Lydia (FC)

Oppia – servant & companion of Lydia, wife of Sergius (FC)

Paul – apostle to the Gentiles, follower of Jesus (FB)

Pontius Aquila II (aka Aquila) – son of Pontius Pilate & Claudia, witness of Jesus's crucifixion, member of senate, friend of Paul (FC)

Pontius Pilate – 5th prefect of Judea, husband of Claudia, father of Aquila (FB)

Priscilla – wife of Pudens, friend of Paul (FB)

Pudens – son of Aurelius & Diana, husband of Priscilla, cousin of Lydia, member of senate, friend of Paul (FB)

Rebecca – Jewish business partner of Lydia in Thyatira (FC)

Rumena – fortuneteller until demon was cast out of her by Paul (FN)

Sejanus – Praetorian prefect, administrator of Roman Empire under Emperor Tiberius (FB)

Sergius – servant & companion of Lydia, husband of Oppia (FC)

Silas – traveling companion of Paul (FB)

Syntyche – part of prayer group at riverbank, leader of Philippian church (FB)

Syzygus – elder of Philippian church (FB)

Timothy – traveling companion of Paul, pastor of Ephesian church (FB)

Unnamed father of Evander – grandfather of Lydia & Janus, merchant of purple cloth (FC)

Unnamed masters of Rumena – men created uproar in Philippi that led to the imprisonment of Paul & Silas (UN)

Unnamed son of Janus – son of Janus & Clelia, merchant of purple cloth (FC)

Valeria – daughter of Lucius & Lydia, wife of Eubulus, mother of Olivia, merchant of purple cloth (FC)

ACKNOWLEDGMENTS

I do not cease to give thanks for you ....
Ephesians 1:16 (ESV)

… my partner in all things, LaVonne,
for choosing to trust God as we follow Him in this faith adventure
together;

… my family,
for your love, support and encouragement;

… Sheryl,
for once again helping me tell the story in a far better way;

… Scott,
for being able to juggle all of your priorities;

… a phenomenal group of friends
(many of whom have stuck with me through all of the books)
who have read an advance copy of this book,
for all of your help, feedback and encouragement;

… and most importantly,
the One who is truly the Author and Finisher of it all
– our Lord and Savior Jesus Christ!

ABOUT THE AUTHOR

Ken Winter is a follower of Jesus, an extremely blessed husband, and a proud father and grandfather – all by the grace of God. His journey with Jesus has led him to serve on the pastoral staffs of two local churches – one in West Palm Beach, Florida and the other in Richmond, Virginia – and as the vice president of mobilization of the IMB, an international missions organization.

Today, Ken continues in that journey as a full-time author, teacher and speaker. You can read his weekly blog posts at kenwinter.blog and listen to his weekly podcast at kenwinter.org/podcast.

And we proclaim Him, admonishing every man and teaching every man with all wisdom, that we may present every man complete in Christ. And for this purpose also I labor, striving according to His power, which mightily works within me.
(Colossians 1:28-29 NASB)

PLEASE JOIN MY READERS' GROUP

Please join my Readers' Group in order to receive updates and information about future releases, etc.

Also, i will send you a free copy of *The Journey Begins* e-book — the first book in the *Lessons Learned In The Wilderness* series. It is yours to keep or share with a friend or family member that you think might benefit from it.

It's completely free to sign up. i value your privacy and will not spam you. Also, you can unsubscribe at any time.

Go to kenwinter.org to subscribe.

Or scan this QR code using your camera on your smartphone:

Printed in Great Britain
by Amazon